KALPANA SWAMINATHAN lives in Mumbai, a few streets away from her detective Lalli. Since *Cryptic Death* (1997), Lalli has appeared in six novels, the most recent being *Greenlight* (2017). Her other novels include *Ambrosia for Afters*, *Bougainvillea House* and *Venus Crossing*, which won the Crossword Fiction Award in 2009.

Kalpana also writes with Ishrat Syed as Kalpish Ratna. Their most recent work of nonfiction is *The Secret Life of Zika Virus* (2017).

I0649538

ALSO BY KALPANA SWAMINATHAN

Lalli Mysteries

Cryptic Death and Other Stories (1997)
The Page 3 Murders (2006)
The Gardener's Song (2007)
The Monochrome Madonna (2010)
I Never Knew It Was You (2012)
The Secret Gardener (2013)
Greenlight (2017)

Fiction

Ambrosia for Afters (2003)
Bougainvillea House (2005)
Venus Crossing (2009)

Children's Fiction

The True Adventures of Prince Teentang (1992)
Dattatray's Dinosaur (1994)
Ordinary Mr Pai (1999)
The Weekday Sisters (2002)
Gavial Avial (2002)
Jaldi's Friends (2003)

Murder in Seven Acts

Lalli Mysteries

KALPANA SWAMINATHAN

SPEAKING
TIGER

SPEAKING TIGER PUBLISHING PVT. LTD
4381/4, Ansari Road, Daryaganj,
New Delhi—110002, India

First published by Speaking Tiger in hardback 2018

ISBN: 978-93-86582-96-6
eISBN: 978-93-86582-94-2

Typeset in Adobe Garamond Pro by SÜRYA, New Delhi
Printed at **Sanat Printers, Kundli.**

Contents

A Face in the Crowd

For
Amla

The trouble with NRIs is that they expect time to stand still in India, and then they think it unreasonable when it won't. Parents age. Unwanted aunts and forgettable uncles are discovered in dire straits. Cousins unheard of since childhood prowl the property, terrifying the grandparents. Then there are smaller, more life-threatening crises: forms to be submitted to prove one is alive, pension arrears to be claimed. Light bulbs to be changed. Ceiling fans to be cleaned. A pickle jar to be opened. Small things which demand a dexterous agility that cannot be managed across cyberspace. Somebody's got to take charge, and that can't always be done across 5,000 miles. Which is why Florentine has such a good job going.

Florentine doesn't call it a job. He's a wiry man of fifty, seldom seen detached from his bicycle, cruising the lanes between eight and lunch time, and then again after dark. If you need him, you just have to call, and he's there in ten minutes to organize your life. Sometimes he notices things that worry him, and leaves them at our door. Lalli and he go back a long way, which is one reason why she finds it difficult to say no to Florentine. The other, more obvious, reason is that she collects curiosities.

Florentine regards me as an intruder. He greets me every time with, 'Accha, you're still here?' But last month, the purpose of his visit was—me.

'I saw your photo yesterday,' he announced. 'I came here to tell you that only. I saw your photo yesterday.' He dusted a chair with a filthy kerchief and sat down gingerly. 'And I am asking what is our Lalli's niece doing in Auntie May's house?'

'But I don't know any Auntie May,' I protested. 'It must be someone else in the photograph.'

'No. It's your photo. So, Lalli, you must tell me what to do with Auntie May.'

'Who is Auntie May?' I persisted.

'Weak in the head, poor thing. Her niece is big noise in New York. She calls me last night. Nancy. Nancy Sequeira—'

'Oh Nancy! We were friends at school. But Nancy was from Bandra, Florentine, that's not on your beat.'

'Nothing like that, I go where I'm called. Nancy may be from anywhere, but Auntie May is just beyond the railway line. Broken-down cottage you must have seen, big Christmas tree at the gate, bent like an old man. Lives alone. Old lady. Takes in sewing. Used to make wedding dresses one time, now it's all readymade.'

'What did Nancy tell you?' Lalli asked.

'Seems Auntie May phoned her seven times last week complaining she's been followed. Nancy got my number from Krishnamurti's son. You remember

Krishnamurti? Fellow who was always misplacing his keys? I looked after him after his brain operation, his son is so grateful, he gives my number to everybody. So he gave it to Nancy. Can you please drop by and do the needful. Request is always the same. So today I drop by, but I'm not sure what exactly is needful. You see, Auntie May is not being followed.'

'No other relatives around, Florentine?' Lalli asked.

'All flown like birds. Come in Florentine, Auntie May says, as if she's known me all her life. Very formal lady, very polite. She makes me sit down, offers me tea. I bring up Nancy. "Yes, that's what I told her," she says, "but it's not exactly true. I'm not being followed. But everywhere I go, I see this face."

'I didn't say anything to that immediately, but she said, "I know it sounds mad, putting it like that. But that's what it is. A face. The same face. Always the same face."

'In such cases, best keep them talking. After some time they run out of petrol, you give them some small bit of news, some gossip, they get distracted, like that. Then next day it starts all over again.'

Florentine took a sip of water and nodded thoughtfully.

'Otherwise Auntie May is quite healthy, keeps the house neat as a pin. Maybe I gave you the impression she's very old. I only call her Auntie May because it's easy. She's not old enough to be my aunt. Maybe a few years older than you, Lalli, that's all. Active.

Tough. Not easily frightened. So why is she seeing that face? I'm at a loss, I don't know what to tell her. And then I see the photo on the piano and think, this is our Sita, maybe she can help.'

'What do you want me to do, Florentine?'

'Maybe, if you have the time, you could talk to her? She might tell you something more, and I can convey at least that to Nancy Sequeira.'

I didn't relish the prospect, but I agreed. After Florentine left, Lalli said, 'It's not like Florentine to be so timorous. I wonder why he didn't probe further.'

'I think he was a bit intimidated by her manner.'

'Intimidated, yes, but not by her manner. Along the railway line he said, didn't he? All the other old houses there have gone. I wonder how May's cottage has escaped so far.'

'Nancy was never a close friend, I'm surprised she saved my photograph.' I frowned. 'I don't even remember what she looked like.'

'Nancy didn't save your photograph, Sita. May did—' Lalli's voice trailed off. She had gone back to her book. I was left with the uncomfortable vision of myself on Auntie May's piano.

***

Auntie May opened the door just a crack and peered at me.

Emboldened or reassured, she opened the door wider and smiled. She was a very pretty woman, even at sixty. Her face was carefully made up, her hair styled. She was dressed in a powder blue blouse and black skirt, both cut beautifully. The black pumps were worn, but polished to a high gloss. This, at five in the evening, when most women her age lounge in a Mother Hubbard.

'Is it a wedding dress, dear?' she asked.

'No, I'm afraid not—I'm a friend of Nancy's—'

'Ah. Come right in!'

Florentine's description hadn't prepared me for the lovely room I entered. It was tiny, exquisite, full of lace and flowers and sunlight from the big windows. There were cushioned window seats. It was like being in a doll's house or a dream. But it wasn't, because there, on the shiny little piano, was thirteen-year-old me.

The photograph was older than I expected. There were five of us, with Nancy in the middle. We had won a prize of some sort—no, wait, it was the inter-school quiz, and that figure standing behind us was surely Hero Harold, the quiz master. Or was it? The photograph had been cropped, amputating Hero Harold across the waist.

'Did Nancy phone you, dear?' Auntie May asked. 'She's been so kind ever since I told her about my trouble. Yesterday a very nice man called Florentine came here, such a helpful creature, fixed the geyser and wouldn't take anything for his trouble.'

'What's troubling you, Auntie May? Nancy said you were being followed.' I decided to leave Florentine out of it for the present.

'No, no, I just told her that because it's so hard to explain on the phone. I expect that's why she asked you to visit me?'

'Yes,' I lied.

'It's a face. Everywhere I go, I see the face. When I go to the market, there it is. At the bus stop, there it is. Last week I went to Dadar, and there it was on the train.' Her voice had risen in distress, her mouth trembled. She dabbed her lips nervously with a lace-edged hanky.

Seeing her distress, I understood Florentine's cowardice. Her hand tightened its grip on mine. 'You don't think I'm mad, do you?'

'No, of course not!' I was lying with facility this morning. 'Could you describe the face, Auntie?'

Her face closed like a sulky child's. 'It's just a face,' she said petulantly. 'Just a face in the crowd.'

'Is it a man or a woman?' I asked.

'It's a woman, a young woman, younger than you. You're thirty?'

'Thirty-five.'

'My! You look much younger.'

'You're very elegant yourself!'

'One tries, dear. One must try. I was raised to believe that. No matter what happens, don't wear your heart on your sleeve. Besides, clothes do make a lady, especially if she's a tailor!'

'Let's get this worry cleared up, Auntie May, then I'm going to bother you with a request.'

'Oh, it'll be a wedding dress, I have no doubt. Pretty girl like you, what are you waiting for? I never had a wedding dress, you know.'

'No?'

'Never had a wedding, so never had a dress! Now Nancy's wedding dress was all her mother's idea. You must have noticed at the wedding, the train looked like a curtain. And the bridesmaids! Pink dresses, can you believe it? Cheap stuff. Twinkle nylon we used to call it when I was young...'

After a decent interval I steered her towards the face again. 'When did you last see the face?' I asked.

'On Tuesday.' Her voice sank. 'I couldn't stand it after that. That's why I called Nancy. Send me somebody, I begged, I can't bear to go out on my own anymore.'

'And she sent Florentine?'

'Yes. He seemed a very decent person. I've asked him to do all the marketing for a week. Then we'll see. Maybe the face will go away by then.'

'When did you first see it, Auntie?'

'Oh, I can give you the exact date. The fourth of May. I had gone to the naka for a loaf, and there it was, staring at me over a tower of bread. I was so startled, I knocked over the display, and the shopkeeper was good and mad, but others calmed him down. That was nice of them, but somehow that sort of kindness really hurts, it makes me feel I've got one foot in the grave.'

'What happened after that?'

'Right then, you mean? Nothing! All that fuss took up some time, and when I looked up again—there was nobody there. I thought maybe I'd imagined it, but that very evening when I went out to get some fruit, there it was again.'

'What did you do?'

'Nothing! I put it down to weakness. It was very soon after my operation, you see.'

'You had an operation? You were ill?'

'Broke my hip. Slipped in the bathroom. I was in hospital for only three or four days, then they sent me home and I had a nurse to look after me. She was here for ten days, very helpful, but you know how it is when you've got used to doing things on your own, there really isn't place for two people in the house. She was supposed to stay for a fortnight, but I got better so fast, I let her go after ten days. I felt bad about it, she had such a hard life, poor thing, but I had to consider expenses too. Especially as I had to get the bathroom done and all.'

'Must have been difficult having workmen in the house.'

'Oh, nurse managed all that, I must say. I give her full marks for efficiency. She got the men, got the job done, left the place spotless.'

'And soon after that you saw the face?'

'April 15th I had the house to myself again, and on May 4th I saw that face for the first time. Do you think it's weakness? I haven't been taking that iron tonic, you know.'

'Have you been eating and sleeping well, Auntie?'

'No, dear. What with all this worry, how can I? Sometimes I fall asleep in front of the TV, so yesterday I asked Florentine to shift the TV to my bedroom, but it kept me awake till the milkman came.'

'I think it's weakness and exhaustion, Auntie. Do you have help with the housework?'

She snorted. 'Help? I'm not used to the soft life, dear. I've been thinking I'll get back to my sewing. Face or no face, a woman's got to make a living hasn't she?'

Despite her optimism, she darted anxious looks at the street as I left, and the lace curtains were drawn close when I turned to wave.

When I got home, I found Lalli packing hastily.

'It's the Jalna matter, Sita. Things are coming to a head and they're making a mess of it. I don't know if I'll be of any help at all, but I must try. They're picking me up at seven. Why don't you grab a lift till Buldhana, and take the bus home to Lonar? You need a break, Sita.'

I rushed to pack before she could change her mind. I needed to get out of the limbo in which I had spent the last month after sending off a manuscript to the publisher. Between now and seeing the book in print, life would be unendurable. A spot of gardening with my parents, and the excitement of watching a new rose might just help. They were awaiting an interesting hybrid, and I could be in at the birth if I stuck on for a fortnight.

I did. The Jalna matter took longer than Lalli expected, and it was three weeks before we returned.

Florentine arrived soon enough to remind me I'd completely forgotten Auntie May. He looked reproachful when I opened the door. 'I made a mistake. I thought Lalli's niece would be like Lalli. Big mistake. Got used to seeing you here. Forgot this was transit lounge for you.'

'Cut out the drama, Florentine,' Lalli snapped. 'You can reproach her niece for whatever's happened to May, but not mine.'

'Look, I'm sorry I wasn't around.'

'Why be sorry? You've got your life. Only Florentine has no life, only everybody's.'

He waited for that to sink in before saying 'Terrible, terrible. I kept thinking if Lalli were here, maybe we can do different. But now it's too late, the story is finished.'

Sick with dread, I could barely ask, 'What happened?'

'Lost her head completely. You know long ago, when we were kids, we used to call her Maddy May. I didn't like to tell you that day because she seemed to have become normal. But it all came back, didn't it?'

'Why did you kids call her Maddy May?'

'Don't remember. She was very pretty, like a

Hollywood actress. Naturally, we boys were going up and down that road all the time. She and her father, only two of them. Father was strict, used to beat her with a stick. Our parents warned us not to look at May because she was mad. That's all I remember of that time. When I came back here twenty years ago, the old man was dead. May had a tailoring shop, doing well, making wedding dresses, but she was private-like. No family, no church. One or two fellows got the push when they tried something.'

'So that's why you were reluctant to question her, and you pretended you didn't know anything about her,' Lalli observed. 'No wonder you tried to get Sita to do your work for you.'

'If you get angry I won't tell you what happened.'

'Suit yourself.'

'Just now you returned? Must be tired. Okay, I'll go now.' And he continued sitting where he was for the next ten minutes.

I made tea to break the impasse and found a packet of biscuits.

'Directly you left, May went crazy,' Florentine began. 'Two days later, she refused to open the door till I shouted out my name. She said that bloody face was everywhere. So I asked her never mind the face, what does the rest of the person look like?' Florentine paused and looked delicately at Lalli.

'Good question, Florentine,' said Lalli the peaceable.

'Very good question. Because you know what her

answer was? Every time the face was on a different person! In the last forty-eight hours, she had seen the face four times. First: woman bringing children home from school. Second: shopping in burqa, veil up. Third: girl plastered to boyfriend on bike. Fourth: ragpicker woman. What was I to make of this?'

'What did you make of it, Florentine?'

'I got scared. I wrote email to Nancy Sequeira, very sorry to inform you Auntie May is mental. Nancy was very good, she phoned immediately and gave me the number of a mental doctor in Santa Cruz. Oho, I thought, all along she knew the story, then.'

The next day, Florentine had persuaded May to accompany him to the psychiatrist in Santa Cruz. May kept telling him on the way that she had seen the face at the bathroom window and had decided not to use the bathroom till it went away.

The psychiatrist told Florentine that May would be fine with some pills and back went May, convinced the face would turn up in the bathroom again.

When Florentine rang the bell at ten next morning, she let him in fearfully, pointing to the bathroom door that stood ajar. The wall was broken. The new tiles had fallen out revealing a cavity—

'But she'd just got the wall fixed,' I protested.

Florentine, rattled, remarked that some people knew everything even if they were never around, before he went on with the story.

There was something in the cavity. May crouched

against the door trembling, as Florentine pulled out a gunny bag disintegrating with grime and age. Its contents tumbled out on the bathroom floor.

A framed photograph. Booties and a baby's frilly dress, and—Florentine crossed himself. 'Skeleton. Baby's bones. Head.'

May had stolen up, and picked up the photograph before Florentine could stop her. She took one look at it and started screaming, 'No! No!' She kicked that pathetic pile of bones, wild with rage.

'After that what else could I do? I called the doctor, called the ambulance, took her to hospital. Maddy May. What to do? I phoned Nancy and told her, let her be in hospital for the present. Nancy is going to come Christmas time, then she can find a private nursing home or something like that, long-term. I locked up the house. Sad story, but what to do?'

'What did the doctor say?' Lalli asked.

'He said her past had driven her mental. That must be her baby, no? Had it secretly. Baby must have died, and they plastered it in the wall to avoid talk. All these years the guilt ate into her, kept seeing the man's face everywhere till it made her completely mad.'

Lalli got up, opened out the newspaper on the dining table and tapped on it invitingly.

Looking sheepish, Florentine produced a plastic bag and arranged its contents on the newspaper.

The faded dress and booties must once have been pale pink. The bones were all jumbled together. The skull alone looked complete, paper-thin, with huge empty eye sockets that glared reproach. And there was that framed photograph.

Lalli laughed. It was her ringing laugh of triumph that bodes danger, not amusement.

Florentine nodded. 'I'll leave it, then?'

'Yes. You can go now, Florentine. I'll let you know what I need by and by.' Florentine, relieved, made a quick exit.

'Come, Sita, let's look at this,' Lalli invited. 'It's your case, after all.'

She stirred the bones around with a pencil. 'Small mammal, quadruped, cat probably. Notice there's no jawbone in the lot? And as for this skull, it's too neat don't you think? Membranes intact. Notice the bleaching. Interesting.'

It was rather pretty, in a gruesome sort of way, a warm ivory hue, the diamond-shaped membrane atop stretched tight as parchment between the delicate bones. Why would—

'Exactly. I knew you'd get it. The bones would have come apart had the skull decomposed naturally. This is a preserved skull—takes some skill to get such a perfect anatomical specimen.'

'You talk as if it were something instructional.'

'It is. That's exactly what I'm telling you—this is a skull preserved for the purpose of teaching anatomy. And the rest of the bones aren't human.'

'But the booties, the dress...'

'Don't forget the photograph.'

It lay face down. I was about to pick it up when Lalli caught my hand. 'How about a guess?'

'Oh, no need to guess, Florentine told us already. It's the face.'

'I need a name, Sita! And only you can give me that name.'

'I?'

'Trust yourself, Sita,' she urged.

I didn't have the faintest. She rummaged through her desk and returned with a large envelope. She slid the photograph face down into it, sealed it with tape and placed it on top of the bookcase. 'Let's look at it after we've solved the case,' she twinkled.

It was generous of her to say *we*. So far I had done nothing beyond pushing Auntie May over the brink.

When I was about to go to bed, Lalli said, 'Give me a day or two, Sita. After that I promise you'll be able to set things right for May.'

'How can anything be set right for her ever, Lalli? She's committed.'

'Oh, nonsense. Two days, and you can establish just how mad May is. And don't worry about Florentine, he gets paid for his goodness, remember? It's a *job*.'

I hardly saw Lalli over the next two days. She came home late, wolfed down dinner and then was on the phone till all hours. Finally, on Saturday morning she told me we could visit May.

***

There's nothing quite as desolate as the psychiatric ward of a general hospital. Anomie fills you at every breath. Empty eyes accuse you. And suddenly, you're the one that's suspect, impoverished prisoner of sanity.

I almost didn't recognize May. It wasn't just the hospital clothes, a horrid green and white floral Mother Hubbard. It was her expression. Her face was a sullen mask of apathy. She responded to our greeting with a grunt and flopped heavily into a chair.

'Do you remember me, Auntie May?' I asked.

She said slowly, 'Nancy's friend.'

'This is my aunt Lalli.'

'Hello, May.'

'Hello.'

'May, do you know why you're here?' Lalli asked. Something in her tone made the green gown and the drab cubicle irrelevant. May sensed it too.

'I'm here because I'm mad.' The words were spoken slowly, with extreme conviction.

'I don't think you're mad, May.'

'Well, good for you. But I know I'm mad.'

'Not true. You have been told you're mad. Do you remember how your trouble started?'

'I saw a face. A face in the crowd.'

'So you did. But you were told you *imagined* the face.'

'No. I actually saw it. Everywhere.'

'You saw it everywhere because it was everywhere, May. Had I been standing with you, I would have seen it too.'

'Why? You mad too?'

'I'm as mad as you are, or you're as sane as I am, and I'm here to prove it to you. First, tell me, is this the face you saw?'

Lalli put a photograph on the table: a young woman, staring angrily at the camera.

May gasped. 'How do you know?'

'It's my job to know things. Now tell me, May, did you break the bathroom wall?'

She shuddered, but shook her head.

'That was not your baby in there, May.'

May looked up sharply, then the light faded from her face just as quickly. 'It is. It was. Doctor said it was. He said I had forgotten and it made me mad.'

'Doctor was wrong.'

'How do you know? Are you a doctor?'

'Yes, I am. Those were cat bones, May. The skull was from the medical college. Somebody put them there.'

May shook her head. 'It's very sweet of you, dear,' she said. 'But it's no use. The photograph—nobody else could have put that photograph there. I did. I must have. You see, *I knew him.*'

'Yes. And *he* remembers everything that happened between you. You may have forgotten, May, but he remembers.'

The film of apathy finally lifted from May's eyes. She looked wary, frightened. 'You know him?' she asked.

Lalli nodded. 'As soon as I tell your doctor the full

story, he's going to realize you're not mad, and let you go home. Do you feel strong enough to do that?'

May seemed uncertain. Then she said, 'I could ask Sister Jacob to stay for a while, couldn't I? I'd feel so much safer that way.'

'Is that the nurse who helped you after your hip operation?' I asked.

'Yes! She was here to see me yesterday, so sweet of her, really. She works here, but in another ward somewhere. I'm sure she'll agree.'

'Good! But let's not bother her right away, May. How about I talk with your doctor today, and you ask Sister Jacob after we have all the papers settled?'

'Okay. You sure the face won't come back? I've seen it twice in the hospital.'

'Of course you have. But you won't see it again, May, except when I ask you to.'

'Mad!' May got up purposefully. 'You and me, we make a real pair. What are they giving you, shock treatment?'

'No. But I could give you one right now, May. I am going to ask you to see the face. Three seconds from now that door will open, and you will see the face.'

'Bah!'

'One. Two. Three—'

The door opened. May screamed.

A young woman in a red salwar kameez walked in and rolled her eyes at May.

'Come on, Auntie, cut out the drama. I won't

hurt you. I didn't know really that I was meant to frighten you, or I wouldn't have done it. Look, I'm sorry, okay?'

She turned to Lalli. 'There. I've apologized. Can I go now?'

'Wait!' May's voice rang out angry and imperious. 'It was you, every time?'

'Oh yeah. Different disguises. It was fun, the money was good. I didn't ask questions. Are we done here?'

'Here, yes. Inspector Shukla will record your statement at the chowki. He's waiting outside.'

'I'm not going to any chowki.'

'Oh, you're going all right, but you can choose— with or without handcuffs?'

I noticed Shukla's gleaming boots and immaculate turn-ups beneath the inadequate curtain. He was right outside.

She went quietly.

May was trembling, red-faced. 'Who is she?' she whispered.

'A two-bit model, hired from a very shady agency. The question is, by whom? I'm going to ask you if you'll come home with me, May, just for today? It may not be safe for you to go home, just now. But you can call Sister Jacob tonight and arrange for her to be at your place tomorrow afternoon.'

'To your house? But I can't impose, dear. I can stay here for one more day, it won't make a difference.'

'No, May. Please come with me.'

'Doctor won't agree.'

'I've spoken to him already. Your discharge card is ready.'

'Please come, Auntie May.' She turned as if she'd suddenly noticed me and touched my cheek gently.

'Isn't that you in the photograph with Nancy?' she asked. 'Is that how you knew?'

Lalli smiled. 'Why, that's clever of you, May. Yes, that's how Sita knew.' Feeling a complete idiot, I helped May pack her bag.

May was fast asleep in my room when we had a visitor, a wizened man, weather-beaten, with a great shock of white hair. His tall frame looked fallen in, shoulders slumped awkwardly, knees bowed.

Lalli welcomed him, but didn't introduce him. 'It's good of you to have come,' she said.

'Not at all. You have given me a chance to set down a burden. Tell me what I can do.' The voice was familiar, a rich baritone I had certainly heard before.

'First, I have something that belongs to you.' Lalli reached up to the top of the bookcase and brought down the envelope containing the photograph. 'Please open it.'

He took out the photograph and whistled. Then he looked up with a laugh and demanded, 'How did you get this?'

The laugh transformed his wizened face. I knew this dashing cavalier with the melting brown eyes—'Hero Harold!'

He stopped laughing abruptly and stared at me. 'Why if it isn't little Miss Know-it-All, grown up!'

'You remember me?'

'Sure. Walking encyclopaedia, 1988. Or was it '89?'

''87.'

'Hero Harold, eh? That's what you kids called me?'

He preened a bit so I quickly said, 'Yes, but in a sarky way.'

'Nothing like a teenager, to take you down a peg or two. Or a teenager, grown up.' He smiled, and I was suddenly unsure of the sarcasm.

'I left in '90,' he addressed Lalli. 'I thought I should tell you in person why I left. I didn't want to—I couldn't tell you—over the phone. And anyway—I wanted to see the old country before it became impossible to travel. I have this muscle disease—'

'Yes, I noticed. Mr Martires—Harold, I'm hoping you'll be able to help us clear up more than May's problem—'

'How is May? From what you said I gathered she was in a very bad way. That was the main reason for my making this trip now. I don't know what amends I can make—' He frowned suddenly. 'How did you get this picture?' He set the photograph down, and I caught sight of it for the first time.

It was a studio portrait of Hero Harold, younger than I remembered him.

'I gave this picture to someone, and when I asked for hers in return, she evaded it with a laugh. That should have warned me. But nothing did. I was crazy about her, simply crazy. Poor May, it broke her heart.'

'Harold, is this the woman you were crazy about?' Lalli displayed a photograph of a dumpy woman in a sari. It was a candid shot, the subject clearly unaware of the camera. There was something familiar about her, but I couldn't place her. She looked no different from many heavy middle-aged women.

Harold didn't think so.

'Yes, it's Gracie. She must be sixty, but she hasn't changed a bit. See that look in her eyes? Unmistakable. So calm, so unafraid, so brave. That's what I used to think then. What an idiot I was.'

'Tell us what happened.'

'1989. This young lady called me Hero Harold just now, and it's true, I had quite a reputation. I was in demand, parties, weddings, any kind of function where they needed a windbag to start off the fun, I was there. Funerals. Regular Mark Antony at funerals was Harold Martires those days. The girls were all mad after me. That's why I chose May when I decided to settle down. Pretty as a picture, but very dignified, a perfect lady. It wasn't easy winning May, but I did. Her old man loathed me. I never could see May without his sitting between us, glaring. We were to be married that December. Then I met Gracie. I had been invited to the Syrian Church in Santa Cruz, open-air event, big crowd. All at once there was chaos. A cow crazed by the traffic charged in, plunging right into the crowd. You can imagine the panic. Then this slip of a girl in a blue sari plants herself bang in the path of the mad beast like a toreador and makes this loud noise that cowherds use, like this.' He sucked in his lips and made the plosive noise used to placate cattle. 'And it worked! The cow calmed down. She talked to it, rubbing its back, then after a while, it trotted off quietly. Of course, all the wiseacres had something to say, but she wasn't waiting around to hear it. She looked at me, instead. And that was it. Man, I was hit worse than that cow.'

A reminiscent silence overtook him. Lalli prompted him gently and he continued.

'Gracie lived with her mother and little brother Jose. Kid had problems—not quite normal—and she hated him, hated having to care for him, clean after him. He wasn't a bad little chap, I got quite fond of him. The mother was a harmless soul. Just an ordinary family. Gracie taught school, earned quite a bit, paid the bills. She got after me to leave May. I couldn't face the old man, so I kept putting it off, till everyone knew. The wedding invitations were printed by then. May became the laughing stock. The old man threatened me with a revolver—luckily, it wasn't loaded.

'Gracie was with me when he turned up, and she managed him as she managed that crazed cow. Walked up to him, took the gun from his hand and pushed him out of the door. "This is it," she told me, "let's get out of Bombay."

'That was fine with me. I had a job offer from a school in Mussoorie—they might accommodate Gracie as well, I thought. She was all for it. And then it all blew up in my face.'

He picked up the photograph and puzzled over it. 'What do you think, Madam? Does this lady look like a criminal to you?'

'Impossible,' I protested.

'That's what I tell myself these days. Maybe my own guilt about May forced me to colour the incident. Let me tell you what happened. Gracie and I were pretty much certain of the Mussoorie job, but she kept worrying about Jose. And then, one Sunday morning when I went over at ten to their place as usual, she let me in with a tight smile. There was a curious tension in the air. The mother was sitting stony-faced at the table. "Where's Jose?" I demanded.

"We needn't worry about him any more. He's gone to his rest," Gracie said.

'I tore past them into the house, and the poor little boy was lying dead in his bed in a pool of vomit.

'"What happened?" I asked.

'Gracie shrugged and smiled slyly. A little while later, she went in to make tea. I asked the mother in a low voice if the doctor had been sent for. She shook her head and put a finger on her lip. Gracie said, "Nobody will say a thing. He was retarded, and now he's dead. Finished. Let's get on with life."

'I said I would go make arrangements for the

funeral, but I never did. I ran home, packed a bag and vanished. I couldn't face the thought that Gracie might have got rid of little Jose, so I ran away. That's what I used to do when I was young, run away. I ran away from May, I ran away from Gracie, I ran away from Bombay. A year later I managed to go to Australia. A lucky break. And, believe it or not, this rascal was recruited into the police! Life's been good to me, better than I deserved. Then last year I was diagnosed with this disease. Slow killer. So when your friend in the Queensland police visited me, I was only too eager to give her all the details. That's my story. Now tell me what I must do.'

'Would you like to meet May?'

'Oh no, no. Anything but that. Couldn't face that, really.'

'Is your family expecting you back very soon?'

'What family? The boys in the precinct are my family. Old reprobate like me can't expect to have folks around him. No, I'm here for a while. I'd like to find out if Bandra remembers me.'

'Oh, Bandra remembers you all too well,' Lalli said drily. 'How do you think we found you? The stories will make your ears burn.'

He laughed. 'They'll be startled then to see how I've changed.'

'Changed? You haven't changed a bit,' Lalli said. 'Has he, Sita?'

I shook my head. 'Just the same hero he ever was.'

'Lalli, I must know now how you found Hero Harold,' I stated flatly as the door closed on him.

'You told me, Sita! That photo of yours with Nancy had pride of place on May's piano. Was it for Nancy? She could easily have framed a better picture of her niece. I assumed the other three girls were like you, strangers to May. But there was someone else in that picture—an abbreviated presence. His picture had been cut across, very likely by the people she got the picture from, Nancy's parents. After the scandal in the family, they wouldn't want Harold in the album! But May had wangled the picture out of Nancy. After that it was easy finding Harold. He's famous in Bandra, they still talk about him. I traced him easily to Australia. The real surprise was when my friend in Queensland, Allora Taree, told me Harold was a respected policeman.'

'So how did the picture Harold gave Gracie turn up in May's bathroom wall?'

'Oh, Sita, how did anything happen to May?'

I heard a door open and May shuffled out hesitantly. She sat dreamily next to Lalli on the sofa and accepted a cup of tea.

'After all these years,' she murmured. 'After all these years, I heard Harold's voice again in my dreams.'

Lalli picked up Gracie's photograph and showed it to May.

'Sister Jacob,' May said. 'Oh dear, I should have phoned her earlier. Have you met her?'

'No, not yet.'

'Oh. How did you get her photo then?'

'You could call her now, May, and ask if she could come in early tomorrow and get the house ready for you. Perhaps make a meal too, so when you move back home, you can have your lunch and a good nap.'

'Okay.'

'Best not tell her anything more now.'

***

Lalli woke me at six the next morning. 'Come on, Sita, let's hurry!'

We shot through the dark lanes of Vile Parle and were at the road parallel to the railway line in five minutes. Lalli parked behind a truck and we walked silently around May's cottage. Lalli climbed over the low wall and I followed. The back door opened to Lalli's light touch and we went in.

'Lalli!' It was Shukla, standing very upright against the wall. 'She's coming in now.'

We flattened ourselves against the wall next to Shukla. Our vantage commanded a clear view of the kitchen, which was, as yet, completely dark.

The lights came on. A stout woman in a sari bustled into the kitchen with a wire basket. Eggs. Butter. A loaf of bread.

A pouch of milk. She took out a syringe from her purse. She stood the pouch upright and squeezed the top edge of it to empty it of milk. The needle gleamed as it slid into the angle of the pouch pinched between finger and thumb. Her movements had the swiftness of long practice, the certainty of a method tested and proved. Injected this way, the pouch wouldn't leak. She hummed as she worked, put the syringe away in her purse. She went to the fridge: the interior was crammed with food. Florentine had shopped well.

It took her a few minutes to find what she wanted. A pouch of milk similar to the one she had just injected. She switched the two milk bags. Still humming, she picked up her basket and left the kitchen.

'Let her go,' Lalli restrained Shukla.

We went back home.

The rest, Lalli said, was up to Savio.

***

At eleven, Florentine opened the door of May's cottage and let in Sister Jacob.

'Better sit down and relax for a few minutes before she gets here. You won't get any rest after that,' he said.

Sister Jacob sank into the sofa and accepted a glass of water. 'That bad, eh?'

'Very bad,' Florentine shook his head. 'Doctors today don't know what they're talking about. In my time this one would have been in the asylum.'

'Poor thing.'

'Wait, don't get up, I just made some tea, better have a cup.' Florentine placed a loaded tea tray on the table, and poured out a cup for Sister Jacob.

'Thank you, but I never drink tea.'

'I thought so when I heard your name. Jacob is from Kerala, I thought, coffee preferred. So I made both. Here, try the coffee, good thick milk and plenty of it.' He handed Sister Jacob a steaming mug.

'What about you?'

'Black tea. Can't digest milk. Don't let it go cold now. Have a biscuit.'

'Where are you from? Goa?'

'Me? Born, bred, buttered and jammed in this city. Not going anywhere else except up or down. Sugar okay?'

'Perfect.'

'How do you know? You haven't touched your coffee.'

'I'll have it by and by.'

'Why won't you drink your coffee, Gracie?' Harold stepped out of the kitchen. 'Afraid you'll die like little Jose?'

Sister Jacob screamed and dropped the coffee all over her sari.

Then she got up and faced Harold in the same manner in which she had faced that cow. 'Who are you?' she asked. 'Who is Gracie?'

'Both questions only you can answer, Kochamma,' Lalli said as she walked in. 'Kochamma Jacob alias Gracie Kuriakose, you should have drunk that coffee and saved yourself what lies ahead. Florentine, can you fix another cup for Sister?'

'Here. Lots of milk,' Florentine held out a cup.

Kochamma knocked it out of his hand and snarled at Lalli. 'Is this a game?'

'Hardly,' Savio chose that moment to enter. He waved a paper at Lalli. 'Exhumation order for Jose Kuriakose. Kochamma Jacob, you're under arrest.'

When the dust had settled down and Kochamma Jacob was arraigned, I remembered why she seemed so familiar. A year ago I had met her one afternoon in the market when she accosted Lalli. That afternoon, I had mistaken her for a nurse. Lalli corrected me, saying she had quite a different profession.

'Oh, what does she do?' I'd asked.

'Murder, mostly,' Lalli replied.

I remembered too that she was Savio's nemesis. Lalli had summoned him from Delhi yesterday, soon after Harold left. Kochamma had evaded Savio at least a dozen times to my knowledge. I only knew that from Lalli. He never mentioned her name. Now at last there was evidence. He hadn't looked so happy in years.

'It was so clearly a personal vendetta against May,' Lalli said. 'May led a secluded life. Who could have hated her so much except her rival for Harold? And who else had access to May's life except Sister Jacob? They had to be the same person.'

'But Kochamma Jacob's notorious, she's into big-time crime. Why did you think of her in this case?'

Lalli laughed. 'I didn't! It was sheer fluke. I showed

the nursing agency our Most Wanted album, and they picked her out for me!'

***

May's back in her cottage now. Last week she had the walls knocked down and two new rooms put in. It might be a while before they're used, but she's keeping them ready.

Meanwhile, she's back to tailoring. The first thing she's sewing is a wedding dress. And this time, it's her own.

The Quantum Question

For
Marise

'Why are we here, exactly?' I grumbled. We were parked on Bandra Sea Face. Seven o'clock on a rainy evening.

High tide. The sea a blue-grey spatter of gall. A curl of corruption in the cold air, sneaking in from the Koliwada, where heaps of drying fish sweat under tarps. The road a froth of mud in a mad hurry.

Only teary-eyed streetlights divided the elements. No other horizon showed between wringing waves and scolding sky.

The place to be was home. On the balcony with a book, fitting accompaniments within reach. For the challenging page, a cup of jeera rasam, argumentative with pepper and garlic, with a curry leaf crisped in ghee to preserve the decencies of debate. For more mindless pleasures, coffee would do. Hot, smooth and sentient, with luxurious nibbles of Lalli's fruit cake. Between pages lurked other delights. The elusive scent of the last rain-washed jasmine on the trellis. And somewhere within the watery curtain, the certainty of birds, dreaming in eaves, in trees.

All these joys traduced for—*this*?

'I think it's the perfect setting for a ghost story,' Lalli said.

I looked askance at Savio, uncharacteristically at the wheel this evening, because it was his junket. He passed me a square of chocolate. His usual bribe, fruit and nut.

Not nearly enough today.

Sighing, he broke off two more squares before answering. 'And that's the bhoot bungla to your left.'

'*That*?'

Even with three squares of chocolate, I wasn't swallowing *that*. *That* was the bhoot bungla everyone knew. It was so much a bhoot bungla, only an ulterior motive could justify it. Films, naturally. For years I had simply assumed it was a kind of permanent movie set. Why else was it still there?

It stood at a slight elevation, as if marking its distinction from the brash new money jostling the road. It was a double-storied house with long verandahs opening through a multiplicity of wooden-framed windows. Very possibly it had a courtyard, a winding staircase with a rose window at the landing, carved furniture encased in cobwebbed cerements, bats in the little tiled gables, and, of course, ghosts. Nobody had lived there in years.

'Look!' Lalli breathed.

The ghost was in residence. Lights glowed on the first floor of the bhoot bungla.

'We're here by invitation,' Lalli said. 'Tell us the story, Savio. I was in Paris all that year, so I don't know anything about this ghost of yours.'

'My ghost was—is—was—a lovely girl. Rupa Bhavnani, the daughter of our physics professor. Six of us were his special students—the rest of the class resented this. They called us the Bhavists. He was a wonderful teacher, and we six enjoyed the problems he set us. Rupa was younger than us, much younger, she had just finished school. Lost a year when her mother died of cancer. I suppose that was a bond between us. I was very fond of Rupa. Delicate as a sparrow, but nerves of steel. I admired her courage when she stood up to her father. Professor Bhavnani was the usual patriarch, tough love expert, girl's place is in the kitchen kind of guy. And Rupa—she hated all that, she just wanted to scamper free of housework. Poor little Rupa, it was a lonely life for her with only their sullen cook for company. She used to wait for Saturdays, because that's when we Bhavists gathered for the weekly quiz at the professor's place. And *that*, Sita, was his place. It was no bhoot bungla then. Just a sprawling old-fashioned family home. The professor's father had built it when he came here after Partition. All of us looked forward to those Saturdays. It was the cook's day off, so there was a spread from Karachi's. Rupa loved chaat. She pecked like a little bird—' Savio's voice trembled, and he gave me another square of chocolate.

This time I did shut up.

'I'll go straight to the day the house became a bhoot bungla. It was a Friday. We were in the canteen, shooting the breeze, when one of the guys who loathed us dropped by at our table and asked, "What are you Bhavists doing here? We thought you'd be in the crematorium, seeing you're family."

'It sounded like a ghastly joke—till we discovered the reproach was serious, and hurtled out in mad haste.

'We reached the crematorium just as the rites were over. My little birdie—' Savio broke down. He put his head on Lalli's shoulder and sobbed his heart out.

It had stopped raining. A pale light wavered, uncertain as memory.

'Right,' Savio pulled himself together and gave me the rest of the chocolate. 'It was horrible, it was tragic, but it was a common accident. Rupa woke up early to study. Professor was already out on his walk. The cook was away, she had left for her village that week—so Rupa decided to make herself a cup of tea. It was a primus stove...'

'I thought those horrors were extinct,' I protested. 'Nobody has those stoves anymore.'

'This was '88. And no, primus stoves are still around. And 23 per cent of deaths from stove accidents are homicidal,' Lalli said. 'Go on, Savio.'

'You can guess the rest. Professor came running back when he saw the house go up in flames. He tried to get in, but Rupa had bolted the front door. By the time the fire brigade guys had the fire under control, she was long dead. Her charred body was found in the kitchen. The entire ground floor was burned down. That was the end of poor Professor Bhavnani as well. He was like a man dazed. He locked up the house and resigned from his post. I never heard of Professor Bhavnani again.'

Savio paused for breath. Everything about him tensed up. 'Last week, I received a letter. By post. You know how rare snail mail's these days.' He handed Lalli a letter from his pocket. She skimmed through it, then passed it on to me.

Hi Savio,

How are you?

It's been a long time since we had a Saturday together. See you at the old place on the 12th, at seven, as usual. Don't be late! Samosas!

Love,
Your little birdie.

'She always wrote with sketch pens, sometimes each word a different colour. She was such a kid!'

The note I held was written in bright blue ink, definitely with a sketch pen.

'I didn't know what to make of it,' Savio continued. 'Postmarked Bandra. Nothing else to identify the sender. I was disturbed—I thought of it as crank mail, but who would play a prank like that? Only somebody who knew me back then. By the end of the day, I had emails from the other five in our group. We had all been out of touch for years. The others too had letters like this one, and each contained some detail pertinent to only the person addressed. So here we are, at Professor Bhavnani's place. It's Saturday, the twelfth, seven o'clock. Shall we go in?'

We were not the first to arrive.

There was a woman hesitating on the doorstep, glaring at a guy who was using his umbrella as a shield.

'Oh Savio! Thank God, you're here!'

She ran down to us and enveloped Savio in a fierce hug, then quickly included Lalli and me in a warm smile that quite belied her earlier look of rage. She took Lalli's hand in both hers. 'You must be The Family. Savio used to carry your picture in his wallet, very smart in uniform. That's what he called you. The Family. I thought you were all his invention—and now here you are, for real. And you are—'

'Sita.'

'Mohini. Savio, the first thing I see when I get here is this warty, loathsome toad.'

The man with the umbrella coughed.

Mohini glared again, then grabbed my left hand and Lalli's right in sisterhood. 'Let's just ignore him. What else can we do to a guy who walked out without a word on his girl? No reasons, no explanations. Just—silence. And that's what you're getting from us—silence.'

Having got that off her chest, she turned to Lalli. 'So you're the reason why Savio joined the police? He was going to be—what? The next Pele, when we last met. God how young we were.'

'Some of us seem to have stayed that way,' Umbrella said.

'And you, I suppose have aged like some rare wine?'

'A fine Muscadel,' Umbrella agreed.

'Oh come out of hiding, you idiot!' Mohini cried, exasperated.

The umbrella collapsed on the instant, revealing a smallish guy attached to a spectacular beard. He bobbed his head at us uncertainly in greeting then looked hopefully at Mohini.

'Meet Darayus,' Mohini sighed.

The banter had gone out of her. She was still holding my hand, unconsciously squeezing it in distress.

Darayus didn't seem afflicted by any such discomfort. He was just planted there stolidly, staring at Mohini.

Luckily, the impasse was broken by the arrival of the others.

Madhuri, heavily pregnant, supported by Aquil. And an impossibly tall guy they greeted as Torry.

Introductions over, Savio and Lalli were crowded with letters. I read them too.

Written with different coloured sketch pens, they were in the same painstaking schoolgirl cursive as Savio's was.

With all the commotion our arrival had made, I was surprised the door hadn't flown open yet, but the house continued its sulk. Apart from the bright glow in two windows on the first floor, the rooms were unlit.

'Ring thrice, that's the rule,' Mohini whispered.

Silence fell upon the group. All of them, Savio included, looked meaningfully at me.

I pressed the doorbell.

Madhuri was almost fainting with excitement. Aquil caught Lalli's look of concern. 'There was no stopping her, she would come,' he murmured.

That was all we needed on a rainy evening. A spectral epistolary, and now a miracle birth in a bhoot bungla.

The door opened on the third ring. An elderly man regarded us with an uncertain smile.

Everything about him was silvery, from his carefully combed thatch of hair, his bristly moustache, his kurta pyjama of grey silk. Certainly festive attire, down to his silver embroidered mojdis. All that elegance was wasted on him, though. He was just a frightened man in a huddle of silk.

The Bhavists soon dispelled his uncertainty with their affectionate and joyous greeting, but for all his hearty response, Professor Bhavnani's eyes continued to look wary, if not frightened.

'I was told to expect all of you,' he began shakily when we were all seated. 'I received a very strange letter.'

'We've all received those letters,' Mohini said soothingly. 'What do they matter? We're here, aren't we? And so glad to see you well, Sir.'

'Well? I've forgotten the meaning of the word.' Professor Bhavnani sighed. 'Grief is an incurable disease.'

'None of us have forgotten Rupa,' Savio said in a low voice.

'You were always her favourite.' The professor smiled. 'She wouldn't want us to be so dismal, and seeing she's summoned you here, I made certain all your old treats would be here. I hope you haven't outgrown them! Come, tell me about yourselves and the adventures you've been having in the brave new world.'

I could see why they had found him irresistible. A tinge of irony barbed his affectionate manner, but there was no doubting his warmth or his interest in them.

The atmosphere grew convivial. Stories unfolded with much laughter as we enjoyed chaat and sweets.

The talk came around to physics. Mohini was the only one who had pursued physics as a career.

'The kind of science you do is beyond a fossil like me,' Professor Bhavnani said cheerily. 'So I'll simply luxuriate in pride without asking questions.'

'As do we all,' said Darayus.

'Arre, Darayus, that daari has grown more than you!' the professor quipped.

'Can't afford a shave these days,' Darayus retorted.

'Set it on fire!' Mohini shot back thoughtlessly.

A brutal silence extinguished the laughter.

Then Lalli's clear voice asked, 'Did you remodel your house yourself, Professor?'

Now why would she imagine that?

Yes, the cozy, if garish, interior of shiny new laminate and soft furnishings was in total contrast to the battered exterior, but it was nothing an army of carpenters and masons couldn't pull off in a week.

To my surprise, he flushed with pleasure. 'Your mother is a very observant lady,' he told Savio. 'Yes, I did every inch of the work myself. I'm a fair carpenter.'

'You've created a new world within the old one. I find that curious,' Lalli said.

'Yes. I wanted no reminder of the old place at all.'

'So you built this shell of wood and laminate. Curious, very curious. A labour of love. Or of despair.' Lalli was being needlessly harsh. 'Took you almost a year to finish it, I see.'

'How on earth do you know?' He drew back as if stung.

'From your hands.' With no ceremony, my aunt reached forward and held his open palm, tracing the callosities with a fingertip. 'More than a year. And today is the first time you're entertaining visitors here. You still find it difficult to live here.'

'Yes.' Baffled, Professor Bhavnani was reduced to monosyllables. The Bhavists were staring with open horror at my aunt.

Even Savio looked embarrassed.

It was up to me now. 'Perhaps that's why all of

you have been summoned here today,' I said. 'The question is—who summoned you? Who wrote those letters?'

'Does it matter?' Madhuri asked irritably. 'I mean, we're all here, that's all that matters.'

'To you, perhaps,' Lalli said. 'What did the sender of those letters want? What did she or he expect of you Bhavists, and of you, Professor Bhavnani? Now that you are here, what do you want to do? What do you want, Professor?'

He shook his head, refusing an answer.

'The letter-writer simply wanted us here together again,' Savio said. 'I think she trusted us to do the rest.'

'Then we must do it, mustn't we?' Lalli rose and looked about the room. 'Perhaps we can start by admiring your curious house, Professor. Will you be so kind as to show me around?'

Helplessly, the old man nodded and walked us through the bright interior.

Lalli was particularly taken with the kitchen, a nasty cube of ice blue laminate and stainless steel, like a futuristic slaughterhouse.

'No open flames, I see,' she observed with an approving smile.

I could feel waves of hate stream off every one of those Bhavists towards my barbaric aunt.

'Thank you for the delightful tour, Professor,' my aunt beamed, unfazed. 'The letters are, of course, self-explanatory. Let me see yours, please.' Her voice was pure ice.

He handed her the letter from his desk, quite cravenly. She passed it to Savio and invited everybody to read it.

The Bhavists looked enquiringly at their professor. He waved them on with a helpless gesture. Really, I was beginning to lose my patience with Lalli. The letter was very terse.

Dear Pappa,

Your students will be here on Saturday, the 12th as usual! Don't forget the chaat!

And at last you will be able to sleep well again.

'It's not signed,' I said.

'It says "Dear Pappa", who else can it be?' the professor said heavily.

'Dear Professor, Rupa didn't write this,' Mohini murmured. 'You know she couldn't have.'

'No, she did, she did!' The old man wrung his hands.

'I thought your daughter was dead,' Lalli said bluntly.

'No, she's alive,' his voice rose querulously. 'How else did she write those letters? She's alive!'

'Curious! A girl who's alive and dead at the same time? Now, what does that remind me of?' Lalli's voice was unnaturally deliberate. Her words tinkled like icicles.

'Enough. You've done enough for today!' Aquil said angrily. 'You're upsetting my wife.'

'Then you had better take her home. In fact, we should all leave now. We have done what we were expected to do. If we haven't, I'm sure Rupa will summon us again.' And with a cold nod to the professor, Lalli swept out of the room. I followed.

'Wait!' It was Mohini.

She caught up with us at the car. 'Why were you so mean to him? Do you have—some history?'

'With him?' Lalli asked. I was shocked to see her actually shudder.

'What got you so angry?' Mohini persisted.

'I was not angry with him. I was—I am angry with all you Bhavists,' Lalli said. 'What has science taught you, Mohini? Ask some questions!'

'Exactly.' Darayus had joined us. 'Ask some questions instead of rushing to conclusions.'

'And what questions are you asking, Darayus?' Lalli asked.

'Just one. Why is that house like an egg?'

'Excellent. I congratulate you,' Lalli said warmly. 'Mohini will explain the physics to you, I'm sure.'

'You think?' he asked in sudden hope.

'Eventually.'

'Excuse me, I'm right here!' Mohini said. 'That's the stupidest thing I've heard today. Why is the house like an egg?'

'In fact it's the only intelligent thing I've heard

today,' Lalli shot back. 'Here comes Savio. Sita, you're driving.'

It seemed as though Lalli couldn't wait to rid herself of that place.

'Well, you certainly rattled him,' Savio remarked angrily. 'Why were you so mean to him, Lalli?'

'That was mean?' Lalli was equally angry. 'He'll find out how mean I can get.'

'Yes, but why?'

'Why? Why were you here, Savio? For your little friend? For her father? Or because the anonymous letter-writer tapped into your curiosity?'

'All three.'

'Then prioritize.'

'Obviously, you were there for the last.'

'You're wrong. My motive was completely different, and it will drag me there again very soon.'

It was a silent drive home.

Savio walked off in a huff.

Lalli stopped me when I started after him. 'Leave him to think, Sita. He needs his space.'

Savio did turn up for breakfast next morning, to my vast relief. Lalli was reading as usual, on the beige sofa. Savio slid to the floor at her feet and rested his head on her knee. By and by I brought in the cake tin, and all was quite right with the world.

'It should have struck me right away,' Savio said.

'What should have?' I asked, but they didn't answer me. 'Shall I—'

'No,' said Lalli, 'not yet.'

That afternoon, we had a visitor.

Professor Bhavnani greeted me with a polite smile and asked if my mother were at home.

'My aunt, actually. Yes, please come—'

'No. You are not welcome in my house!' Lalli said over my shoulder. 'What do you want?'

'Something, anything. Anything to end this. I know you can help me. All your questions yesterday—help me, please! My daughter said—'

'Ah yes, the daughter who is both alive and dead. Go home, Professor. I have nothing to say to you.'

'Have some pity for an old man—'

'I'm an old woman myself. Pity is cheap.'

'Then what do I deserve? Tell me that.'

'Like all of us, Professor, you deserve the truth.'

'Will it end my suffering?'

'I don't know. Perhaps your daughter will tell you what to do.'

'You're laughing at me now.'

'Not at all. I do believe, in all honesty, that your daughter will show you the way.'

'Lalli, you can't be serious!' I said when the door had closed on the pathetic old man. '"Your daughter will show you the way?" This from you?'

'As I said, Sita, I honestly believe she will.' And nothing more was to be got out of her that day.

***

Savio received another letter. This time the message, written with a hot pink sketch pen was very brief.

Saturday 19th, 7 p.m. Be there!

The other Bhavists had got invites too.

It was a sullen knot that gathered at Professor Bhavnani's doorstep on the 19th.

Aquil and Madhuri were missing. The baby had arrived last night.

On the third ring, Professor Bhavnani appeared. If he had seemed silvery on our first visit, he was all steel now. His face had lost its folds and was a tight mask of deeply etched lines. He stared at us with burning eyes.

'One more of those bloody letters. I got one too. Which of you is playing games?'

'We'll soon know,' Lalli said smoothly, stepping forward.

He shrugged. 'Come in, all of you.'

The house was as bright and garish as it had been last Saturday, but there was no evidence of forthcoming hospitality.

We sat down on the hard shiny sofas.

'Can I see your letter, please?' Lalli stretched out her hand imperiously.

He gave it to her with a look of pure hate.

Mohini said, 'I'm sorry you're being disturbed like this, Sir. Savio will see that the culprit is caught.'

'I doubt it,' the professor said flatly. 'We will go on meeting like this, to no use, till I die.'

'Oh years and years for that, Professor, don't you worry,' Torry spoke perhaps for the first time.

'Still the same Torricelli, I see,' the professor permitted himself a smile.

'Still get those vacuum headaches, Torry?' Mohini asked with a wicked smile.

'Only when I look at you.'

Behind the general laughter, Darayus whispered to me that Torry was the only real genius in the group. 'Math freak. He's the one who showed me the egg.'

I remembered his conundrum now and asked, 'Yes, what was that all about?' But he hushed me with a look.

Lalli had just said something that had silenced the room. 'I'll repeat my question to this group of physics students. A quantum question, isn't it? A dead girl who is simultaneously alive—'

'Schrodinger's Cat,' I said.

The others looked at me in surprise, as if I had no right knowing a hoary physics conundrum. Man puts live cat in sealed box with lethal stuff: an hour later, the cat could be either alive or dead—common sense, right? But nerds call it quantum mechanics.

'That's a bit disrespectful,' Mohini said.

'Just a little bit,' Darayus amended. 'The analogy is inescapable. But to what end?'

'It leads us back to Rupa. What is she trying to tell us? We'll simply have to ask her.'

'Oh please, not a seance—' Mohini squealed.

'In a room full of rationalists? No, let's do something more realistic. Let's ask the person who knew Rupa best of all. A few questions, Professor, and we can set all this to rest once and for all.'

'You can? Somehow I doubt that,' he sneered.

'Let's talk about little Rupa. Tiny—but brave, you said, Savio?'

'Oh, full of guts,' Savio said sadly.

'Little spitfire when she got angry,' Mohini laughed through sudden tears. 'We adored her. Oh, she was such a baby.'

Professor Bhavnani shut his eyes in a sudden spasm of pain. His words emerged in a thin wail. 'Yes, she was such a baby, just a child. How could she understand?'

'True,' Lalli's voice was low and mesmerizing. 'How could she understand your torment? Impossible.'

'Yes! Impossible. It was impossible.' He took up her words eagerly.

'An impossible situation. An impossible moment. It all happened like this…' Lalli snapped her fingers. 'And then it was done. It was over. It would have been over, all over and past and behind you, if only—'

Professor Bhavnani's voice rose in a powerful lunge. A wordless scream of anguish.

'If only…'

As Lalli's voice trailed off, Mohini asked in alarm. 'What's that noise?'

There was a distant knocking.

'Perhaps it's Rupa at the door,' Lalli said. 'This girl who is alive and dead all at once.'

'Oh she's dead, no doubt about it. We were at her funeral. We carried her ashes to the sea,' Torry said.

'Did you really? What is your name, by the way? You can't go through life as Torricelli. It's insulting,' Lalli frowned.

'Yes, it's a bit painful. Thanks for noticing. The name's Pradeep.'

'Watching a body being cremated and sifting the ashes afterwards is no evidence at all,' Lalli said. 'Especially in this case, where cremation was an overstatement. The body was charred beyond recognition, wasn't it?'

'What are you saying?'

'Just this. The quantum question was as relevant that distant evening as it is just now. At that instant, while you were sifting her ashes, was Rupa alive or dead? She was both, I'd say, just as she's now.'

'I see what you mean!' Darayus said suddenly. 'But how do we solve the conundrum?'

There was a sudden crashing sound.

The Bhavists leapt to their feet.

Lalli held up a restraining hand. 'Please, no distractions. We're here to help Professor Bhavnani, remember? Let's answer Darayus with another question. How do you solve the conundrum of Schrodinger's Cat?'

'By opening the box.'

'As long as the box is sealed, quantum superposition is a possibility. Isn't it, Professor?'

He nodded miserably.

'One lives in hope. But for how long, Professor?'

'What is all this about? What sealed box?' Mohini quavered.

'Darayus, explain the egg,' Lalli invited.

'No, it's Torr—Pradeep's idea.'

'Of course, how could any mathematician have missed it! Tell us, Pradeep.'

'The walls of the house enclose a circular space. But you can see immediately that the perimeter of the space in which we stand is not circular at all. The old house was a circle. The new house is egg-shaped. Granville's egg, actually, but never mind that. An egg-shaped space fitted inside a circular space.'

I tried to visualize it. The garish laminated walls dazzled me. The yellow cushions glistened like fresh yolks. I thought of the stone walls of the house crowding this brittle shell—

A thundering crash, this time too loud to be ignored.

'Let's go,' Lalli's voice rang out. 'I think Inspector Shukla has unsealed the box. Will you do the honours, Professor?'

He sank down on his haunches, his head between his hands, shaking with dread.

Savio hauled him to his feet.

Between Pradeep and Savio, Professor Bhavnani

assumed the vertical, but his head was still sunk on his chest.

'Walk!' Savio's voice had never sounded so ruthless.

They practically dragged him forward. We followed Lalli into the corridor, just in time to see Shukla emerge in a cloud of dust. His hair was matted with cobwebs, and for once, his ivory teeth were not on display. The wall behind him had a gaping hole.

He nodded in answer to Lalli's questioning look and stepped aside.

The broken wall seemed to open into another room, but it was just a recess that led to a bolted door. Rust, grime and cobwebs had made the seal near hermetic.

'Behold Schrodinger's Box!' Lalli said. 'Shukla, give Professor Bhavnani the crowbar.'

But the professor shrank against Savio, clutching at him.

Savio shook him off and took the crowbar from Shukla. In two furious strokes, the bolt gave way, and Savio kicked the door open.

The mephitic air that swelled out is impossible to describe. It was not merely cold and foul and dry, it was *ancient.*

Shukla switched on a powerful flashlight.

Before us was a small storeroom, the usual annexe of an old-fashioned kitchen. Little more than a wedge between ceiling-high cupboards. The small window was now just a scab on the dim wall. And that's all I saw till the roving beam came to a stop over a dark heap against one of the cupboards.

This time the howl of grief that rang out was—Savio's.

His huge frame cut off my view.

I turned to look at Professor Bhavnani. He was as intent as the rest of us, craning for a look beyond Savio's solidity.

'Move aside, Savio, let him see,' Lalli's tired voice was little more than a sigh.

Savio staggered out. I took his arm. He turned blind eyes on me.

Professor Bhavnani approached the dark object on the floor.

Then he turned to Lalli and said with great aplomb, 'I was right, wasn't I? She was dead all along. What a relief. Thank you!'

'Your thanks are a little premature. We don't know yet when she died. But we will, when Dr Qureshi has finished his examination. Take him away, Shukla.'

'Wait!'

Savio shook me off and stepped forward, very close to his old teacher. 'Why? Why did you do this to her?' he asked with that unnatural calm that scares me to death.

Profesor Bhavnani laughed. 'Why? What else could I have done? What would you have done in my place, Savio? Ask your mother. She's a smart lady, she seems to know everything. She'll tell you. Let's go, Inspector. I think I'll sleep well tonight.'

***

'Tell us,' Mohini pleaded.

We had been sitting for almost an hour in that garish living room. Lalli had withdrawn into a galactic distance, responding to questions with no more than an angry shake of her head. But now, perhaps realizing the only way she could get her solitude would be by breaking her silence, she said, 'It's a sordid story, but all too common.'

'If this is Rupa's body, who was cremated that day?' Darayus demanded.

'The missing member of that household. The woman who usually made tea for the professor before he left on his walk. That morning, the cook told him she was pregnant. I'm presuming that's what she told him. I can't think of anything that could have enraged him more. I imagine it like this. As the water boiled, she turned around and told him she was expecting his child. Fatherhood? Marry the maid? Oh no, no, not for our urbane professor. She may have threatened to expose him. What a scandal that would be. How could he endure it? The next step seemed completely logical to him. He grabbed the keg of kerosene, flung it on her, struck a match, and left the kitchen to go for his walk.

'It would all have been over, but he had forgotten his daughter.

'And there she stood, right behind him, books in hand, a horrified eyewitness. He tried to explain—probably. But what could he say? The cook was already a pillar of flame, the fire would spread in minutes. Meanwhile Rupa—valiant, honest Rupa—was screaming things no father should ever hear. So he picked up the heavy iron skillet from the counter and lashed out at her. Rupa fell stunned to the ground. He pushed her into the storeroom, threw in the skillet after her, bolted the door, and stole out of the house through the back door, free to enjoy his morning walk.'

'But—' I could hardly bring myself to say it.

Darayus did. 'But Rupa was trapped in that storeroom.'

'Yes. Bhavnani absolved himself easily. The house was aflame, and he only noticed it after, say, half an hour. Once he called the fire brigade, his duty was done. He had tried to rescue his daughter, but he couldn't get into the house, and then when the charred body was found, he fell on it with despair, ignoring the locked door of the storeroom. A most convenient cremation. With the charred house shut away, insurance money collected, life could begin all over again.'

'Maybe Rupa died the instant he hit her,' Mohini said.

'I doubt it. She must have been just stunned—woken up minutes later, choking in the smoke, helpless to escape. If she screamed, the roar of the flames muffled her cries. A terrible death,' Lalli shuddered.

'You're wrong!' Mohini decided. 'The letters! Who wrote them?'

'Mohini, think! What happened to Bhavnani? He stayed on in denial. In his mind, Rupa really was Schrodinger's Cat. But age caught up with him. Consumed with guilt, he returned to the house. In a desperate measure of denial he constructed this new shiny egg, working every inch of it with his own hands, as he told you. Those calluses on his hands are a measure of his desperation. He had erased the old house, but he still couldn't live in the new one. He was tired of running. He did what every criminal eventually does. He forced himself to face his crime. He had to open the sealed box. So he wrote those letters. Savio was his real hope—I was just his lucky bonus.'

'But you knew almost at once, didn't you?' Pradeep asked. 'You went for his scalp right away.'

'I knew before I entered the house. Savio described Rupa just as we arrived. A lively little girl, brave with dreams, who could never be the docile homebody her father wanted. Such a child would never attempt to make a cup of tea for herself. If the cook wasn't home, she would wait for Pappa to do it. The cook's sudden trip to the village was also too convenient for comfort. A charred body? I've seen too many to believe in them! Then, once I entered the house, the egg that Pradeep described was immediately apparent. A new oval space within the older circular one. I asked myself, why? What lies in the space between? The answer was obvious. Schrodinger's Cat.'

'But why did he send us the second letter? Why send for us again today? What had he intended to do if the police hadn't broken down the wall?'

Lalli laughed. 'I sent this second round of letters. Didn't you notice his surprise?'

'He felt remorse,' Mohini decided. 'You helped him repent, Lalli.'

'Like hell I did' Lalli's voice was harsh with bitterness. 'I just beat him at his own game.'

The Sixth Pandava

For
Shubha

'We've been invited to a book burning,' Lalli said. 'If we hurry we can get there by ten past.'

I was halfway down the page. I had skipped lunch to get through this chapter and didn't relish the interruption.

'Ten past what?' I asked.

'Ten past murder.'

A book burning—*murder*?

Lalli doesn't use murder as a metaphor, but when it's a *book* in question...

The book was Parikshit Joshi's *The Sixth Pandava*. The original in Hindi, *Ek aur Pandav* had passed without comment, but the English translation had right-wing zealots frothing at the mouth.

Lalli slid a bright pink flyer towards me. It exhorted (in Hindi and in English) all anguished Hindu hearts to unite at the very threshold of the criminal who had written this offensive book. Devoted cadets had patiently gathered thousands of copies before they could corrupt the weak-minded, and at exactly 7 p.m., these books would be torched as an act of purification. Brothers and Sisters, be there!

'I've hunted high and low for a copy, but none of the bookstores stock it,' I grumbled.

'You should have asked me.'

'You've read it?'

'Of course. Someone sent me a copy to anguish my Hindu heart.'

'Didn't know you had one.'

'I have a lump of muscle that goes thump and doesn't suffer fools gladly. Hurry!'

Why? She couldn't expect to stop them, surely?

'It's nothing short of murder, I agree,' I said. 'But why hurry?'

Halfway to the door already, she threw up her hands in despair. 'It's the golden moment, Sita! Ten past murder. You should know, you've been there often enough. These last few years, oftener than me!'

As I hurried, I ran over all the times I had arrived on the crime scene ten minutes past murder. The body didn't tell me much, but that's because I always wait for Dr Q to explain.

'It's not about the body,' Lalli uncannily read my thoughts as I slid behind the wheel. 'Kataria Street.'

Santa Cruz East, off the main road. Hell at this hour. Incensed with the message, I had ignored the address on the flyer.

'Second lane off Kataria Street,' Lalli offered. 'Ground floor, Asha Niketan.'

An old building, then. Nivas, Niketan and Sadans are near extinct, replaced by villa, palazzo, mansion, and even chalet in recent years.

'If it's not about the body, why is ten past—'

'*Drive!*'

I smelt smoke the moment I parked in Kataria Street. As we turned into the lane, we were both coughing.

A crowd choked the lane and a sooty cloud billowed overhead. That was expected. What we did *not* expect was the silence. At least a hundred men and as many women jammed the lane—and not a murmur to be heard. The lane was lined with trees, but that didn't cut off the view from the second and third floor balconies, all full of people riveted on the spectacle.

An unaccountable nausea overcame me. I would be sick any moment—

I turned to Lalli—but she had vanished.

I heard a harsh cry of outrage.

In the moment it took me to recognize my aunt's voice, I identified what had made me gag. Earlier, I had smelt burning paper. *This* was the reek of burning flesh.

I pushed my way forward.

As people let me through, they stepped back a little, in the same trance-like silence, still staring right ahead.

Now I stared too.

Lalli was bent double at the edge of the conflagration, tugging at something heavy and unyielding. I couldn't see what it was, for all that smoke. With a tug that almost toppled her, she pulled out something. At that instant, the pall lifted and I saw what it was.

A flaming pair of legs.

The feet, splayed and lurid, stuck out from a column of fire.

The next instant a wall of flame slid over those legs, leaving for one brief moment more, the feet still visible. And then, they too were engulfed.

Another pillar of fire toppled over, and I realized this, and the earlier one, were *books,* whole stacks of them, aflame.

The crowd drew back as Lalli straightened up and faced them with a look of calm contempt. Then she turned and walked up the steps to the door.

The right-wingers had kept their word—the bonfire had been lit practically at Parikshit Joshi's threshold. The brass nameplate on the door gleamed red. The windows, tightly shut and curtained, were so begrimed they had evidently not been opened in years. It was the only flat in the building that opened on the street.

I looked up. All the balconies of Asha Niketan were empty. A twitching curtain here and there betrayed a covert audience.

The door took a while to open. The woman who faced us was about fifty. Her bright salwar kameez contrasted oddly with her dingy appearance. Her broad pasty face was apathetic. The eyes, incurious, slid away after their initial look of enquiry. She let us in without a word and led us down a small passage into the living room. She threw herself down on the sofa she had evidently just quit and waited for us to speak.

Lalli took the chair next to her. 'Is there someone with you, Mrs Joshi?'

She shook her head.

'Children?'

'In college.'

'Hostel?'

She nodded.

'Is there someone I can call, friend or relative?'

She shut her eyes, as if focusing on something immensely difficult. 'Have they gone?'

'Who?'

'The crowd. The books must be ashes by now.'

'How did your husband—'

'Stubborn. Very stubborn man. I told him don't go out, but he wouldn't listen. Opened the door and stood on the steps reading aloud from the book. He expected me to stand there with him, I know. That is my place always. I stand by him, always. But today—I was just tired…very tired…So I came inside.'

'You shut the door?'

'Yes, of course. The noise was unbearable. I had a headache. Migraine, I suffer severely. They kept jeering and mocking him. It was unbearable.'

'What happened after that?'

'They stopped shouting, and I knew.'

'What did you know?'

'It was over. It was over at last.'

'How long ago was that?'

'I don't know. I wasn't looking at the clock.'

'What were you doing?'

'Watching TV.'

'So when the noise stopped, what did you do?'

'Nothing. My serial was going on, very critical episode today, so when the noise stopped, I could concentrate. The crowd would leave now, I thought.'

'What about the fire?'

'What about it?'

'Did you call the fire brigade? Ambulance?'

She looked puzzled. 'What for?'

The doorbell rang.

I had no trouble recognizing the man who greeted me with a very courteous namaste. Kantilal Gera's ingratiating smile was everywhere in the city: he was the party boss. The book burning campaign was his brainchild.

The fire had been put out. Smoke stung my eyes. I watched two men throw down a tarpaulin over what was left of Parikshit Joshi.

'Our boys have put out the fire,' Kantilal Gera said in the unctuous lilt common to his kind. 'The police will be here shortly, but don't worry, I am here, I will take care of everything.'

My silence disconcerted him enough to realize I was not family.

He grew even more unctuous. 'A terrible accident. I must see Mrs Joshi.'

Who was I to stop him? I led him in.

At the sight of his earnest face, Mrs Joshi began sobbing into her hands.

'A terrible, terrible accident,' Kantilal Gera said, engaging Lalli's glare.

'Was it?' Lalli's voice was pure ice.

'Why? Don't you think it was terrible?'

'Terrible, yes. But not an accident.'

Gera nodded with sudden wisdom. 'I see your point of view. Suicide. But you are mistaken. We had no intention of attacking Joshi Sahib. Only his book. The book was our target. Just one hour ago he made a phone call saying he would withdraw the book. At the last moment he saw how grave his error was and he deeply regretted it. He made the ultimate sacrifice. May his soul rest in peace.'

Mrs Joshi looked up abruptly. 'No need to call the police, please. What is over is over. I am not interested in blaming anybody. I only want to be left in peace.'

Gera leaned forward confidentially. 'Leave it to me. Leave everything to me. Your suffering is unimaginable.' He leered at Lalli. 'Take good care of her.'

'Why?'

Startled by Lalli's response he dithered, then narrowed his eyes and demanded, 'And you are?'

'Lalli.'

'Sorry?'

'Don't be. That's my name.'

'Relation?'

'No.'

'Friend?'

'Not particularly.'

'Then why are you here?'

'For the same reason as you.'

'Good. Good.' Kantilal Gera had the politician's genius for mining advantage out of adversity. 'You understand then. Sentiments are hurt. Religious sentiments. My sentiments. *Your* sentiments.'

'Not mine.'

'No? Ah. You are minority. Muslim? Christian? Parsi? You know many think our party is against minorities. We're accused of being anti-Muslim, anti-Christian, but that is absolutely not true.'

'I agree completely. Your party is neither anti-Muslim nor anti-Christian. It is anti-Hindu.'

'Sorry, I didn't hear that clearly. It sounded like anti-Hindu.'

'That's what I said. Your party has subverted, not to say perverted, the religion of reason and plurality into a weapon of hate. Millions of people who were born Hindu don't recognize anything your party says as their religion.'

'You are not a Hindu, so you cannot speak.'

'That's fast becoming your manifesto, isn't it?'

'Why are you arguing like this?' Mrs Joshi cried out. 'My husband is dead!'

Shukla chose this moment to make an entrance.

Gera quickly assumed hauteur and waited to be acknowledged.

Shukla didn't waste time. His ivorine grin looked

particularly malignant as he requested Gera to accompany him to the chowki.

'I can make a statement right here,' Gera responded. 'I was not a witness to the accident, Inspector. I was summoned after the tragedy.'

'That also we will record,' Shukla said equably. 'Abetment to suicide, Section 306—'

'Oh no, Shukla,' Lalli interrupted. 'Make that 300!' *Murder.*

***

Parikshit Joshi lay on a marble slab, his black legs and arms frozen in restrained violence, braced back, powering up for a punch. He had breathed his last defying the world.

'Poetic, but untrue,' Lalli murmured behind me.

I *hate* it when she reads my thoughts.

'Why untrue?' I demanded.

'That's just the effect of heat on muscle protein. Makes every burnt body look like a boxer.'

So even that small dignity of a final defiance was to be denied him. Still—*murder?*

'If it's not about the body, why are we here?' I asked.

Dr Q answered that as he plunged a needle into the blackened torso and withdrew a vial of blood. 'What am I looking for, Lalli?'

'I'll tell you when I find it.'

'I thought you wanted *me* to screen the blood for toxins.'

'So I did! Let's match our findings in an hour.'

'I can't possibly have the results in an hour,' Dr Q protested.

'I can,' said my aunt.

To my surprise, she insisted on driving back to Parikshit Joshi's house.

The morning mist, acrid with smoke, hadn't cleared yet. It was just eight o'clock. An hour later and the press would be all over, but the lane was still asleep.

Apart from the police cordon around a charred patch, nothing betrayed this as the scene of extreme violence a few hours ago. The ash and debris had been cleared away and the area hosed down by Gera's 'boys' against police orders last night, the constable posted there told Lalli.

'What could I do?' he shrugged. 'They were only cleaning up. They were not committing a crime.'

'And what about the man being burnt alive?' I burst out. 'Was that not a crime?'

'He wrote bad things about *Mahabharata*. It was his destiny.'

Lalli stood listening stonily. The emptiness of her eyes startled me. She made no remark but moved swiftly to the door.

'It all depends on the sink,' she said. And ignoring my puzzled look, she rang the bell.

'I'm busy,' Mrs Joshi said when she saw us.

But Lalli had her foot in the door. 'Is your daughter here?' she asked.

'No. What's the use, don't come now, I told her. She is with my brother in Pune. I would have gone also, but that Inspector said I have to wait till the body is released. That is not my responsibility, I said, but Gera Sahib said better I stay.'

So he was Gera Sahib now.

'I would like to help you sort that out,' Lalli said.

After a long silence, Mrs Joshi let us in.

Even her back looked apathetic as she led the way to the living room. She collapsed, as before, into the sofa and stared at us in glazed enquiry.

'Your migraine's bad this morning,' Lalli said gently. 'Have you had some tea?'

'No. Who is there to make tea? I have to wait till the bai comes. Eight-thirty. Who knows, she may not come today.'

'What about your neighbours, will they be around?'

'What for?'

'Did you have something to eat last night?'

'Gera Sahib sent food. Chinese.'

'Let me make you a good strong cup of tea and some breakfast. No, Sita, you keep Mrs Joshi company. I'll call if I need help.'

I had never seen my aunt commandeer another woman's kitchen before. It's domestic violence at its basest, but Mrs Joshi didn't turn a hair. She merely burrowed a little deeper into the cushions and began telling me about her migraine.

I must have switched off at some point, because when Lalli's voice rang out, Mrs Joshi was in full spate.

'—six tablets is too much, I told him, give me something else, but no injections. Needles I cannot bear. So he gave me drops.'

She kept talking. 'I'll bring the tea,' I muttered and made my escape.

The kitchen was a nightmare.

Low-ceilinged, ill lit, it was the natural habitat of *Rattus rattus*. Sure enough, a pair of beady eyes ogled me across the filthy mesh of the window screen. The air stank. The shelves were stacked with dusty bottles, containers, tins, most of them missing lids. A shiny regiment of roaches filed past on parade. A gecko that would soon be a minor dinosaur, completed the zoo.

In the midst of all this squalor, my heroic aunt stood contemplating a blocked sink.

'Sita, can you make her some tea?' Lalli asked.

'Of course, but why are you cleaning her filthy sink? Lalli—you don't have to do that.'

'Not planning to. The sink's nothing. You should have seen the trash can.'

'Does anything, anything at all, smell worse than dead Chinese food?' I gagged.

'I thought it was a body,' my aunt said blithely, 'and it's not Chinese food. It's a solitary rotten potato, can you believe it? And maybe the dead rat behind the stove.'

I screamed and jumped back.

'Don't worry, I've got rid of it. There's milk and bread in the fridge. We did promise her breakfast.'

'You did. Let me do the sink, you take the stove.'

'No, I'm almost done here.'

That's when I noticed she had piled up a stack of plastic bags on the counter. The bags, I recognized. Lalli's handbag was never without these thin polythene sleeves, so convenient to bag evidence. The evidence in this case was revolting. It looked more like the bleb and ooze of decay than yesterday's lunch.

The dead genius evidently moonlighted as cook. Mrs Joshi's career seemed mostly migraine.

Mrs Joshi sipped her tea and pushed away the cup petulantly. 'Sugar. You've put sugar in my tea.'

'I'm sorry, you don't—'

She made a vomity sound. 'I can't bear sugar. And I don't eat toast. Bring me khari.'

'Where do you keep it?'

'Where do you keep it in your house? Same place.'

I could have told her we don't keep khari in the house. Or I could have said, go fetch it yourself. Or I could have stalked out. Instead, I picked up the tray and returned to the kitchen.

Lalli seemed to have finished her researches. She drifted between various outposts of filth aimlessly. A teacup had been added to her stash of samples.

'Can you spot the khari? She can't swallow toast, and sugar nauseates her.'

'Does it now? That's interesting. Okay, the case is complete. There's the khari,' Lalli pointed to a grimy bread box atop the fridge. It rattled desolately as I brought it down. Just the one biscuit. I put it on a plate and we went back to the living room.

Mrs Joshi laughed when she saw the tray. 'You want to starve me or what?'

'There was just one biscuit in the box.'

'As expected.' She made a face. 'Such an unreliable man. Knowing there's only one left, he should have ordered new packet, no? But not Parikshit.'

'Just because *he* doesn't eat khari,' Lalli murmured. 'Men!'

'See? You understand. So your mister also?'

'Don't ask. If I were dying, gasping for water, he'll shout "Lalli! I can't find a glass! Where do you keep them?" So then I will have to totter to the kitchen and pour myself that final glass of water. And at least then you'd think he'll let me drink it in peace? Not at all. He's likely to say, "What gives you the idea you're the only one that's thirsty?" So then I'll say, okay, drink this, I'll have another. And then he'll say, "A man can't find a moment of peace in this house— what were you saying before we got so thirsty?" And *then* if I remind him I'm dying, he'll say, "Not *now*! Dhoni's just won the toss."'

Lalli's rapid-fire narrative of her marital woes had me distracted for a bit, and I missed what Mrs Joshi said in reply. I noticed, though, that my aunt was examining a small bottle on the crowded table at her elbow.

'Your migraine drops, I think? Have you had them this morning?'

'Six p.m. Two drops at six p.m. with a cup of tea and two khari.'

'So yesterday—'

'Oh, don't ask about yesterday. I want to forget all about it.'

'Naturally. So they rang the doorbell just when Mr Joshi had brought in your tea?'

'Yes. He was grumbling as usual, something or the other about the book. And he kept saying there was no sugar in his tea. How much sugar that man ate, baap re. Better stop, I told him every day, or you'll soon be diabetic. That started him off grumbling again, the sugar wasn't sweet enough. So I said, you go bring the sugar here and let me put it in your tea. So he went to the kitchen to get the sugar—'

'Wasn't it simpler to carry his cup into the kitchen and add the sugar there?'

'You or I might have done that, but not Parikshit. He wanted *me* to stir in the sugar. He used to say the sweetness in his tea was the taste of my hand—but that was when we were younger.'

Lalli sighed heavily. 'Everything was different then.'

I hate my aunt when she takes on this martyred identity, but Mrs Joshi grew fonder of her every minute.

'Ours was a love marriage,' she confided. 'His family was very humble, nobody even acknowledged them.'

'Of course, Mr Gera and you are old friends?'

'His family is very well known. Our families are

very close. His father objected to my marriage, but I was young and foolish. And my parents gave in.'

'At that time you shared Parikshit's views?'

'Yes, what do we know at twenty or twenty-five? We can live by our ideals then. In a few years life teaches us that ideals won't fill your stomach. For me, it was too late, but I have taken good care my children won't make the same mistake. Do anything you like in life, I've taught them, but don't end up like your father. This is my only rule.'

'So they haven't read his books?'

She laughed. 'I'll tell you an open secret. *Nobody* has read my husband's books.'

'What about you?'

'Earlier, I used to. Then there was still hope. But the last few years—his books have earned nothing. We have survived on scraps, magazine articles, reviews, that kind of thing, how much do they pay? Two kids in college, tell me, am I expected to starve them? And this last book—it was too much.'

'You've read it?'

'No. I can't read anything these days. My migraine makes it impossible. But I warned him. Don't write, don't publish. Gera Sahib said the same when I sent—'

She frowned and shuffled some papers absently.

'When you sent him the manuscript—or maybe the advance copy?' Lalli asked.

She nodded. 'Parikshit got very angry when he knew they had a copy. Why not, I said, a book should be read. It was what he always said, you know. A book is a book only when it is read. So he could not argue.'

'So yesterday you were expecting trouble because of the posters?'

'The flyers, the posters, they made Parikshit laugh. I said laugh now, you'll be crying afterwards. Then at five-thirty, my son called. He's in engineering college in Vashi. He told his father the same thing. He told him he had disowned him. You're not my father from this moment on, he said. I don't blame him. The book has made his life hell in college. They don't even call him Amal anymore. He is addressed as Pandav or Number Six. Did Parikshit even care about his son's suffering? After that Parikshit phoned Sukriti, our daughter, at my brother's place. She refused to talk to him.'

'Gera told me Parikshit withdrew the book.'

'That was the plan. But Parikshit refused to make the call to Gera and in the end, I had to call him.'

'And by that time the crowd was here already?'

'Yes. Parikshit came back with the sugar, and I handed him the cup when the bell rang. He carried his tea to the door. I also followed him. The crowd was shouting *Parikshit Joshi murdabad!* A big heap of his books was piled on the pavement. That's what I remember most, the scent of new books.'

'What did Parikshit do?'

'He walked down to the pavement, picked up a

copy and returned to the top step. He opened it and started reading aloud. He had a very loud voice.'

'Did he finish his tea?'

'Yes, he drank it all in a gulp, and handed me the cup, as if I were his servant.'

'And like a servant you took it to the kitchen and rinsed it out,' Lalli said dreamily.

'Do you know I've never done that before in my life?' Mrs Joshi wondered aloud.

'And when you got back from the kitchen, he was on the top step, still reading from his book?'

'Yes, by then they had set the books on fire. It was too hot, the wind blew the heat right at me. He turned to me and said, "See, they have lit my pyre."'

'And what was your answer?'

She laughed. 'After twenty-five years of his drama, I knew the dialogue by heart. I said what he expected me to say.' She leaned forwards and spoke earnestly, with great distinctness. 'When he said, "See they have lit my pyre," I answered, "Why hesitate? Go and lie down in it."'

'And then?'

'And then what? I came inside. It was getting late. My serial had started already. So I shut the door and came inside.'

'But he was on the top step.'

'I shut the door and came inside,' Mrs Joshi repeated absently as though she hadn't heard Lalli.

The doorbell rang.

'Gera Sahib,' she said with some satisfaction.

'We'll see ourselves out,' Lalli smiled.

Shukla was at the door. Behind him stood Gera, with his entourage.

Lalli said, 'Please follow me into the kitchen.'

The place felt even more dismal with all of us crowding in. The rat scurried away. The gecko clicked ominously.

'This is the filthiest kitchen I've ever been in,' Lalli remarked cheerily, her back to the sink. 'The moment I entered this room, the case was complete. This is what I saw.' She stepped back, letting the audience take in the blocked sink piled high with dirty dishes, spilt food and garbage. 'But there was one more detail—'

From her bag she took out the tea cup in its polythene jacket.

'This tea cup stood at the very edge of the sink. A clean tea cup, rinsed out—and luckily for us, not very satisfactorily. Now why should somebody have washed just one tea cup? Why not add one more dirty cup to the mess? The answer was obvious. I just had to ask Mrs Joshi for the details.'

'I never said anything,' Mrs Joshi's voice rang out angrily. She elbowed her way to the centre of the kitchen and confronted Lalli. 'I never spoke a single word to you.'

'I don't understand,' Gera said hotly. 'What kind of game is going on here?'

'The name of the game is murder,' Lalli said

grimly. 'Mrs Joshi, I taped our conversation, but even without that, we have enough evidence. I have this.' She brandished the cup and returned it to her bag.

'You're making a mistake,' Mrs Joshi said. 'It's true I put the drops in his tea, but that was just to keep him quiet. It usually works well.'

'You're in the habit of doping your husband with your anti-depressant medication?'

'It's for migraine.'

'No doubt.'

'I take two drops only for migraine.'

'But for your husband you used more, right?'

'Common sense. I had to keep him under control.'

'You've done this before? What was the effect it usually had on him?'

'It made him giddy. Within ten minutes he would lie down and fall asleep.'

'So that's what you did last evening?'

'That's all I did.'

'Then why did you wash his cup? You've never washed a thing in your life, you mentioned with pride. Why did you wash this one? Why not leave it there for the bai?'

Mrs Joshi stared at Lalli sullenly.

'And then, as he stood on the top step reading, right in front of the roaring fire, you shut the door on him, with a push, toppling him into the flames. That is what you did.'

Mrs Joshi turned furiously on Gera. 'You said you'll take care of everything! You promised—'

'I have no idea what you're talking about,' Gera retorted. 'Inspector, Madam, I don't know anything about all this. We were only concerned with Joshi's book. We have nothing to do with his domestic situation.'

'No?' Lalli asked. 'Who's been paying the college fees for Amal and Sukriti? Why did you telephone Amal and ask him to keep away?'

'I'm not answering your questions. This has nothing to do with me or the party, we don't want any more involvement. It was unfortunate that Joshi Sahib took his life in repentance, but we are not in any way responsible.'

'You can tell us all this at the chowki,' Shukla said. 'With or without handcuffs, take your choice.'

'Do you know who I am?' Gera blustered.

'Not yet. But I will find out.'

The pavements were thick with onlookers as Mrs Joshi and Gera were driven out in the care of Shukla and his men.

As the jeeps moved off, the crowd began to shuffle away.

'Wait!' Lalli's voice rang out.

She walked to the top step where Parikshit Joshi had read his last pages, and held up her hand for attention.

'You're here for news, so let me give it to you. Last evening, some of you watched me drag the body of Parikshit Joshi from the fire. I was too late. He was dead already. You will read in the papers tomorrow that his blood was full of a drug that made him lose his balance and fall into the flames. The court will decide if it was accident—or murder. But after examining his body this morning, I have some news for you. We now know that his body was in that fire for at least ten minutes before he died. Ten whole minutes, in full view of more than a hundred people, who simply stood here watching him die.'

She held up her hand again to stem the murmur of protest.

'No doubt you had your reasons, very good reasons too. I know you didn't come here to watch Parikshit Joshi burn. You came here to watch his books burn. This book in particular. *The Sixth Pandava*. You must have been told that it is a corrupted version of the *Mahabharata*. Is it? Listen to this and judge for yourselves:

"Five good men silently watched an atrocity, and I was silent too. I speak now, from my bed of arrows, but you, you who have heard that old story again and again, why did you condone us? Are you another Pandava too?"'

Murder Prêt-à-Porter

For
Kitty

My aunt Lalli collects curiosities.

In the natural order of things, aunts collect curios, and uncles, curiosæ. But Lalli is interested in the unnatural disorder of things. And so she collects curiosities that will, inevitably, lead to murder.

This time, though, it was I who noticed the curiosity.

I sat next to a serial killer on the bus yesterday. I knew he was on his way to do what he does, and there was no way I could stop him. And now it was up to me to find the body.

'What are you looking for, Sita?' Lalli asked eventually, and with reason.

The living room was snowed under with newsprint. I'd been devouring my multilingual stash since breakfast—and not a body in the lot. English, Hindi, Marathi, Tamil—the *Inquilab* alone stayed pristine and aloof, awaiting Dr Q. All, all of them, had disappointed me.

I looked up from the *Dinamani* to meet Lalli's quizzical look. 'It's not there,' I muttered.

'What isn't?'

'The body.'

'Body as in—' Lalli's sentence hovered delicately.

Need she ask?

What other sort do we discuss in No. 44, Utkrusha-B, Adarsh Road, Vile Parle East?

The address was cogent. I expected the said body to turn up on our bus route. It was my first time on 355. I usually ignore the bus that trundles heavily laden from the backwoods of Malad to the mysteriously named Achanak Nagar. In fact, I hadn't been on a bus since I moved in with Lalli. An unexpected squall hit as I was trudging home with groceries in brown paper parcels, we Parlekars being totally committed to biodegradability. I never would have taken that bus otherwise, and landed up seated next to a serial murderer.

And now I couldn't find the darned corpse.

'Actually it's not so much a body as a blouse,' I explained.

'A *blouse*?'

'With the body in it, of course. The body appropriate to the blouse.'

'You're raving, Sita,' Savio observed. I hadn't heard him come in. I was glad to see he had brought Dr Q along. The *Inquilab* was my last hope.

'Why so many newspapers, Sita? Opening raddi shop?' Shukla materialized, slightly out of breath. 'Lalli, you are wanted immediately in high fashion murder.'

Savio explained, 'Leslie Xander asked for you, and then there was the usual phone call that gets the

ACP in a sweat. Xander's a big name evidently. You know him, Lalli?'

'I knew him when he was plain Alexander. What's he done now?'

'He's found a body in his studio. Doesn't know the victim. Door smashed in, no robbery, nothing to explain why a stranger would choose to be strangled in his studio.'

'Is the body wearing a blouse?' Lalli asked.

All three men looked shocked.

'Simple pant shirt,' Shukla offered.

'Not your body, then, Sita,' Lalli sighed. 'Let's go anyway.'

Nobody had time for my story on the way, they were too busy telling Lalli theirs.

Leslie Xander's line in prêt-à-porter could be seen in every mall—but very seldom on the street. His specialty was ethnic comfort: at least that's what his label said: EC by Xander. His one-piece salwar kameez was a newsmaker last year. It looked like the real thing till you had to go to the loo. I knew at least one woman who had emerged after an hour's struggle with the garment in shreds. Another had bravely ripped off the pants and walked out in a dress.

But perhaps Xander wasn't meant for us proles. He had quite successfully dressed Hollywood, by transforming saris into gowns. An airy Maheshwari, weighted with a kundan kamarband had seen the red carpet at Cannes, and a lilac and gold Banaras tissue had been transformed into a fishtail gown at the Oscars last year.

The man himself appeared regularly in the bin liners that come free with the news. He was utterly repellant, not so much physically ugly, as sartorially challenged. His signature guise was a white lurex body suit accented with a low-slung belt, variously embellished. To an opening he once wore a cod piece, described by the fashion press as a *metrosexual langote*.

This then was the man who had asked for Lalli.

Xander had opened his studio this morning at eleven as usual, only to be confronted by something most unusual.

Seated at the cutting table, was a stranger. Leaning back in his chair, he was apparently considering his next move in a game of Scrabble. One hand lay palm down on the table. The other dangled, tightly closed. His head had the tilt of either deep sleep or deep thought, and that made Xander notice, at last, the loops of electrical cable that lashed him to the chair.

Xander palmed the chest for a heartbeat—and felt nothing. He called the police, and when they arrived, he handed them the phone. The voice at the other end was not one the officer could disobey.

'Get Lalli,' it said. 'Clean up the mess.'

Things got messier, when we arrived ten minutes later. I didn't mean that to happen, but what else could I do?

Head Constable Kale took us straight up to the

studio, a glass-walled shed with skylights. But for the large central cutting table and the dummies scattered by the wall, it was devoid of furniture. There was just one chair at the cutting table, and that was occupied.

As I caught sight of the dead man's face, my mouth went dry. I tried to speak, but no words came. The next moment, his face was obscured as the force crowded him.

I told myself I'd made a mistake. A natural one. I'd been thinking of nothing but that face for the last twenty-four hours. It had kept me awake all night.

Savio and Shukla moved away, and the dead face confronted me again.

I hadn't made a mistake.

It was the right man.

But then I caught sight of the Scrabble board, and I knew right away we had the wrong body.

***

'Sita, are you okay?'

I was lying on the floor with my legs propped on a strange object. A ring of anxious faces peered down at me. Between them, I caught sight of the corpse. It was looking at me too, in a politely pop-eyed way.

I got up hastily. The strange object rolled away and I realized it was a dummy, knocked off its pedestal.

Kale produced the obligatory glass of water. As I sipped, the day returned to focus.

I turned to Lalli, and explained, 'It's the right man, but the wrong body.'

'Why?'

'Look at the board, and you'll see why.'

But to explain the body, I had to get them to listen to my story.

'I sat next to him on the bus yesterday and he's a serial killer and it's no use convincing me otherwise,' I said all in one breath.

Shukla was grinning all over his face. Lalli silenced him with a look.

'Why was he a serial killer, Sita?' she asked. 'What did you notice about him?'

I shook my head. The body in the chair blocked off my memory of his face. He looked different somehow. Death had altered the geometry of his features by obliterating purpose. He looked harmless now, a little shocked, but incapable of malice. And yet—

'It's not as if he looked malevolent,' I said slowly. 'He was just so *tense*.'

'Twitchy? Edgy?' Savio asked.

'No, not what I'd call twitchy. He barely noticed me. He had the window, and at his stop, he had to go past me. By then I was so terrified, it took me a moment to move to make way for him, but even that didn't register. He met my eyes without really seeing me.'

'He was absent? Preoccupied?'

'The opposite, actually. He was intent. Occupied. Focused. Terribly, terribly focused.'

'On what?'

'On his book.'

'He was reading?'

'Yes. No. He was *following* a book. He could barely read.'

'A book about blouses?' Lalli asked.

'A notebook. School exercise book.'

'Slow down, Sita, try and relive the moment,' Savio suggested.

'Start earlier,' Lalli said. 'Arrive at the moment.'

'It was ten rupees!' I burst out. 'Do you know I paid ten rupees for—for this!'

I rummaged in my bag and came up with the small square of paper the conductor had swindled me with.

It wasn't even *paper*. It was coated with some kind of evil polymer that made ink break into a cold sweat and slide off the edge, leaving nothing more definite than a smear.

'Ten rupees, and it's smaller than a Band-Aid!'

'Ten rupees is for diesel and driver, not for actual ticket,' Shukla frowned.

'No, Shukla, for me it is. I'm paying for *paper*, to write on.' It's always hard explaining my lust for paper. A proper bus ticket is just the right size for a four-line story, and there are dozens in the aisle.

'Even four-line story is impossible on bus ticket,' Shukla protested.

'Oh yeah? I'll give you one right away:

They loved
He lied

She shoved
He died.'

Lalli cut in smoothly, deflecting Shukla. 'Right, so you were good and mad and that made you notice things. It always does. So what did you observe?'

'I thought the guy next to me was a student, and now I realized he couldn't be. Fine lines at eye and mouth, slack jaw, stray grey fibrils in the brown frizz above his ear. I noticed a sheen of sweat on his cheek, a tremor in the fingers that fumbled hesitantly at the book on his lap.'

I noticed these things, and should have let them go. Instead I had waited to see if he would open that book.

He did.

It was a school exercise book, with flimsy soft covers. The first twenty pages or so of the 100-page notebook had been torn out so clumsily that the back pages had begun to slip their moorings. Going by the careful cursive on the cover, the book had served Heena, Std 4-B, in its earlier career.

My neighbour read slowly, page by page, tracing each inked line with a trembling finger, which, I now noticed, had an ardently cultivated nail. It was long, and so dramatically curved, that its bevelled edge curled like a cassowary's talon.

Then I began reading his book and was soon too engrossed to bother any more about the nail.

'Was it just one nail that was long?'

'N—no.'

The index was the cassowary talon, but the middle and ring fingers had longish nails too. And wait—the left hand that gripped the book had long nails too.

'Sorry for the interruption. Do go back, Sita.'

My neighbour had turned three pages so far. Each page was titled with a woman's name, misspelt in English. The writing was very different from Heena's calligraphy, a laboured, uneven script, the square letters, all capitals, etched in blue ballpoint.

The first three names were MANGL, SVETTA and ZHARIN.

Beneath each name were drawings of sari blouses, four to the page.

The patterns were the sort your average Ladies' Specialist calls *fancy*. The drawings were peculiar. They did not emphasize the things tailors generally drew—neckline, buttons, sleeves. Nor did they have the panache of a designer's imagination. The lines were staid, even stolid. Each drawing was a statement, complete in itself. There were no measurements linking the blouse to the name on the page

Some had directives inscribed in the same laboured hand: *Parpal band, ribin, sort slivs, hux.*

So far (he had got to page eight, Syra). I had no idea what Mangl, Svetta, Zharin, Eshvarya, Joti, Anjli, Vendi, or Saleen looked like. All I could gather was that each woman either desired or deserved a certain blouse.

His finger traced the words hesitantly. It was much surer over the drawings.

His nervousness grew as he turned the pages. A tic galvanized his right eyelid.

The talon began tapping each drawing. He swallowed painfully every time he turned the page. There were ten pages in all, finishing with Vylit and Pael. Then back he went to the first one, flipping pages back and forth as if he were memorizing—what? The pretty seductive patterns or the pretty seductive women who would wear them?

I told myself he was on his way to find these women, to deliver the blouses. Then I glanced at the floor. There was no bag between his feet. All he carried was this pattern book.

The book would lead him to Mangl, Svetta, Zharin, Eshvarya, Joti, Anjli, Vendi, Saleen, Vylit, Pael. Having found them, what would he do?

As if in answer, his finger hovered over *Zharin*. With a predatory swoop, the cassowary claw ripped right across the straggling blue letters. A moment later, he seemed to rue the action. He tried to smooth down the jagged tear in the paper. His left hand gripped the window rail hard, his knuckles blanched.

I knew then what he would do very soon to Zharin. He had gifted her the prettiest blouse. Mentioned the colours too. Butterfly-back, *rani*. Slinky halter, *mango*. Strapless cake frill with a sexy tie, *firdosi ribin*.

He licked his lips, wetted his finger on the tip of

his tongue and pressed it down hard on the tattered *Zharin*.

It was all I could do to keep from screaming. Why did I even make that effort? I should have screamed and got it over with. It might even have stopped him. But I didn't because one part of me, the saner, reasonable part, told me he was just a harmless guy.

He was on his way to an interview. He was a Ladies' Specialist on the verge of taking the plunge into high fashion. Mangl, Svetta, Zharin and the rest would catapult him from Parle to Paris. Or not. I wished I could wish him luck. I wished hard, but I couldn't because—

'Because the saner part of you is nuts,' Savio finished for me.

'Exactly. I *knew* he wasn't going for an interview. He was going to hunt down every one of those women and murder them.'

'And yet you didn't scream,' Lalli observed. 'Where did he get off the bus?'

'Petrol pump.'

'And you stayed on, till you caved in at the signal and jumped off at the last moment and ran all the way back to the petrol pump,' Savio unnerved me by saying.

'How do you know that?'

'I know you. And did you find him?'

'No, of course not. And I was left with this terrible guilt. I couldn't tell you. I didn't have a shred of evidence. Nothing at all, just that book, and the look on his face. There was nothing I could do.'

'Except wait for morning and furtively check the newspaper for bodies,' Lalli said. 'After you got home, what did you make of it all, Sita?'

'Questions kept battering me.' I had written out those questions in my notebook:

Why had he written those names in English, a language he didn't know?

Why weren't there any measurements?

Why did his anxiety verge on panic as he reached the end of the book?

Did Zharin try on the butterfly-back while he waited outside?

Did she complain the blouses didn't fit?

Did he feel insulted, cheated, enraged? Was that the trigger to his madness?

Once we found Zharin, how could we warn the rest?

'I see what you mean, Sita,' Lalli said. 'Right man, wrong body.'

Dr Q, Savio, Shukla and Kale were back to buzzing around the carrion. Which reminded me—

'Where's his book?'

Lalli strolled over to the body to check. She returned to my corner where I was still crouched like a foetus between sternly geometrical dummies. I found them daunting. They were made of some eternal faux metal, not a scratch or a dent on their lightweight perfection.

'No book. Nothing on him, except a pen. You should take a look at that. Pockets empty. The murderer probably took his wallet. His nails have been very recently cut, index ring and middle fingers clipped to the quick.'

'Why would he do that?'

'Oh I don't think he did. The murderer did that.'

'Why?'

'We'll find out. By the way, Sita, he was not a tailor.'

'That was my point, exactly!'

'But I'm not sure he was a mass murderer, either. Dr Q puts the time of death around twelve hours ago, which means he was killed at midnight. Strangled— with cable, probably, there's miles of it around. So either a murder of opportunity, or else the murderer felt at home here. I see what you mean about the Scrabble board.'

'You agree then, it's the right man but the wrong body?'

'Give it a moment. They're about to shift the body now. Let's take another look at the Scrabble board before we question Xander. Well? What do you see, Sita?'

I'm sure by now you agree the board had had nothing to do with the body, but I had to spell it out for Lalli. 'Lalli, the man didn't know English. He wouldn't spend his last moments playing Scrabble.'

'Would you?'

'Yes, if I could use it to name my murderer. But he didn't do that for two reasons—he wouldn't have been familiar with a Scrabble board, and he had a pen, didn't he? If he had wanted to write his last words, he could have. His hands were free. He could have written on the table top, on the board itself—instead of this elaborate effort. Anyway, none of the words on the board are relevant.'

'Here's the pen from his shirt pocket.' Lalli picked it up and scribbled on a piece of paper from her bag. Nothing appeared. She unscrewed the barrel. The refill was crusted and dry.

Nobody had written with this pen in a long time. It was a cheap jotter, the sort you can buy for two bucks.

Lalli found a safety pin, dug it into the refill and wiped it on the paper. The pin left a black powdery smear.

The book, at any rate, had not been written with this pen.

'So the pen didn't work. There's nothing to tell us he tried to write with it.'

Lalli moved the Scrabble board. On the green baize of the table were a few faint indentations.

'We can dust that for prints,' Lalli remarked.

'Even if he did try to write, it wouldn't have been in English. And it wouldn't even have struck him to use Scrabble.'

'From your perspective, yes. But what if he did know English?'

'Not possible. He struggled over that book. Those pages were written by someone who knew the language only at a very basic level.'

'Why was it written in English at all then, in a language he was not comfortable with?'

'Exactly what I've been asking myself since I got off that bus.'

'It's obvious, isn't it?'

'Not to me.'

'It was written by someone who was not comfortable with English for someone who was.'

'Writer and reader spoke different languages?'

'Not necessarily.'

Savio and Shukla joined us, putting an end to the discussion. 'Kale's bringing in designer man and wife,' Shukla said.

Xander was not wearing either his white bodysuit or the metrosexual langote. He was dressed in a sloppy black tee and khaki shorts. His bullet-shaped head wagged a small greasy ponytail. His large teeth protruded when he smiled, giving him a look of uneasy mischief.

He smiled now, greeting Lalli. 'How nice to see you, Lalli. Thank God you're here. Now everything will go smoothly. No mess, no delays. I can't tell you how critical today is, I just can't afford a glitch of any sort! Now tell us what we can do to help you spirit the body away. May I present my Muse, Xara?'

Lesser men have wives.

Xander's Muse was tall and willowy, with a mop of orange curls upheld by a fantastic pile of plastic fruit. Her face was a work in progress. The eyebrows were shaped ready for take-off and the eyelids painted in zebra stripes.

'We have a show at three, all this is so messy,' she sighed. 'Do you have any idea who the poor man is?'

'Do you?' Lalli asked.

'Never seen him in my life. It was sheer luck that Xander came here today—'

'I thought you said you opened the studio at eleven everyday?' Lalli interrupted.

'But there's a viewing today. We keep the studio shut the whole day. We empty it out the previous afternoon after the rehearsal.'

'You rehearse here?'

'Just the fittings. I do those myself,' Xander said importantly. 'The devil's in the details, they say. I check every piece personally. I check the models too. Everything must be in sync, perfectly streamlined. I can't bear the slightest discordance—it upsets everything. That's my job at rehearsals, to see nothing offends my eye.'

'So who would have been here during the final fitting?'

'Our models—Xara's one of them, as you can see. Myself, and if we need any finishing touches, Masterji.'

'Masterji being your tailor?'

'Hey, no, no. Let's get this straight. I'm the tailor here. Darzee, me. Master does the hooks.'

Hux.

The word jumped out of nowhere. It jumped out of my memory. 'Does Masterji carry a notebook?' I asked.

'Of course not, he's illiterate!' Xander snapped. Then, turning his dental charms on me, he added, 'And you are?'

'Police,' Shukla said, the only compliment he's ever paid me.

'And how many models were here yesterday?' Lalli asked.

'Eight, including Xara.'

The studio had been empty, bare, cleaned up when they left at six o'clock. The Scrabble board had been put away in its box and left on the table.

'Is that its usual place?' Lalli asked.

Xara smiled indulgently. 'Yes. It's his warm-up, isn't it, Xander? He can't think without it. The moment he's at the table, he's shaking out words.'

Xander blew her a kiss. 'Logophile, me.'

***

Xander and Xara lived in Santa Cruz. They had spent the evening at a friend's place, and didn't leave till well past midnight. No, nobody else had the keys to the studio. Xander opened and locked up everyday. This morning he came by to check on a detail—and found the door open. The lock had been forced—no great matter that, it was only an ordinary one.

'So last evening there was nothing major in terms of fitting and alterations?' Lalli asked. 'I imagine you would have finished up much later, otherwise.'

'Wonderful!' Xander rolled his eyes. 'See Xara, that's why I asked for her. You're absolutely right, Lalli. Each creation was a winner. Perfect cut, perfect fitting. Lucky for us too—our Masterji took the day off yesterday.'

'Why?'

'No idea. Just didn't turn up. These people are like that, you can't blame them, they're not professionals, but when it comes to piece work, hooks, buttons, a quick tuck and hem, we can't do without them, can we?'

'Of course we can, darling,' Xara said. 'No one sews a button quite like you.'

'Thank you, my love. Now, if we're quite finished here, I'd like to get my show going. There's a press conference after the viewing. It's my magnum opus, the collection that will transform the Indian woman into the international icon of femininity.'

'Oh!'

'As always, my inspiration was Xara. I dare, she wears.'

'Are we invited?' Lalli smiled.

'Absolutely! You would never before have seen a sari blouse attain such sophistication, such mystique, such innocence and such power. Power!' He grabbed the air with his fists.'Woman power! Front row, ladies. You boys are welcome too.'

The boys scowled.

Lalli walked the charming couple to the door.

'Where does she find them?' Savio muttered.

Shukla raced to the window to spy on designer man and wife, and knocked over another dummy in his haste.

Struck off its pedestal, it rolled ignominiously onto its pharaonic breasts, exposing the cavernous interior. Savio pounced on it with an exclamation.

Stuck deep in the faux metal shell was a curled up notebook.

They drew back, leaving me to open it. It was exactly as I recalled, except for one detail. Inserted between Vylit and Pael were three nail clippings. One of them, longer than the rest, was curved like a claw.

To my surprise, Lalli was more interested in the nail clippings than the book. She turned them over delicately with the point of her penknife. Then she walked over to the table and joined Savio at the Scrabble board.

'There were two people at Scrabble,' Savio said. 'The tiles are placed in two distinct ways—some have been pushed around, some have been carefully placed.'

I saw what he meant. Some of the words were aligned, the others had at least one letter out of sync.

'So out goes your theory that the dying man sent out a message,' I remarked to Lalli. 'It's not even certain he made any of these words. Two others could have played.'

'Xander makes all of them play every day,' Kale said. 'He says it improves their English. But I've checked on their routine. The board is always put away in its box when they lock up. So this game was set up later.'

Lalli said, 'Then we can be certain who the two players were. The victim, and the murderer. The victim wanted to convey a message. But the murderer wanted us to ignore it. So he made new words. To begin with, he—or she—placed the tiles without much thought. But when he stepped back, the contrast was evident, so he moved some tiles out of alignment. Now we can't tell which words were made by the victim, and which by the murderer.'

'It's of no use then,' Savio grimaced.

'I wouldn't say that. Would you, Sita?'

I was clueless. So, apparently, was Shukla.

'Nobody is playing games when about to die,' he informed us. 'Also, after murder, why should murderer continue game? If he is worried, why not put game back in box? Simple solution.'

'Maybe the murderer didn't think of that simple solution,' Lalli suggested. 'Only the intelligent apply Occam's razor.'

Shukla was not letting that pass. 'About that, I do not know. Deceased is poorly shaved, I agree. But intelligent minds are using other brands also. Personally, I am Gillette and what is objection?'

Lalli gravely patted his cheek and assured him it was above reproach.

'We should question models now. At least then we will know when this man arrived, who spoke to him, who saw him leave—'

'Go ahead, Shukla. Catch them before the show. But you'll find that nobody's seen the dead man before. And they're not lying either. Kale, what about the Masterji?'

'No name, no address, no phone number. Even if they know, it's beneath them to admit it. Old Muslim man was the best Mister and Mrs could do. Typical of these types.'

'Designers?' I wouldn't have thought Kale knew enough about fashion folk to form an opinion.

'Celebrities! Masterji slaves here day in and day out and they don't know a thing about him. To them, he's just a sewing machine.'

Lalli laughed, her ringing dangerous laugh. 'Kale, you've solved the case.'

'Me? Impossible.' He looked pleased, nonetheless.

'Kale, remember the quarry case in Malad, the one in which a blind man led us to the murderer?'

'Afghani?'

'The same. Find him. Ask about Masterji in Afghani Mohalla. I may be wrong, but it's worth a try. Can you find out? Who's on that beat?'

'I'll check—'

'They probably know him as Masterji in the mohalla. Just in case they don't, tell your man to ask who plays the rubab there.'

'Rubab?'

'Afghani guitar. Sita says the dead man was a musician.'

I?

Kale hurried away to make his phone calls.

'Naturally, the murderer cut off his nails,' Lalli smiled.

'The murderer cut off his nails because he was a musician?' Savio sounded perplexed.

'I don't think the murderer knew that. He cut off the victim's unusual nails simply because they were unusual.'

I felt a stab of sadness as I realized that cassowary talon had been cultivated to make music, not murder.

'Why rubab?' I asked. 'He could have twanged any stringed instrument with that nail.'

'Index and middle fingers, ring finger too. Sarod or rubab, I'd say. Sarod players often have grooved nails. Rubab has a more staccato note, no *meend*, so the string doesn't cut in. Usually, the left hand stops the strings and a plectrum is used to pluck on the right, but some players don't use a plectrum. They prefer the nails.'

'I've never seen the instrument.'

'Oh you've seen it in pictures—Mughal miniatures of Tansen. Sen-e-rubab, it's named after him. But if you want to hear it, Afghanistan is the place. Many Afghanis migrated to Bombay in the early 1900s to work the quarries—Andheri, Malad, Kandivli. That's the connection, but it's no more than an educated guess. Also, our bus route begins at that mohalla, in Malad. Chances are, our rubab player lived in that mohalla. If that's Masterji's book, I'd say the dead man was sent here yesterday by Masterji. So there's a good chance Masterji lives in that mohalla too.'

'That explains the book,' Savio annoyed me by saying. I was still trying to work that out.

He explained, 'Masterji wrote the book for the dead man. He didn't write in Urdu as this guy didn't read the script. But he spoke the language—Masterji wouldn't have written *firdosi* otherwise. The book was written to educate the dead guy about those blouses before he got here.'

'So that's all he was doing? Learning? Memorizing? Why was he so tense?'

'Pity the guy, Sita. He had to learn all that stuff by the time he got off the bus. Not everybody can reel off verse by the yard like you.'

I let that go. Savio is a Ghent to Aix man. Any poem more subtle is lost on him.

'I agree with Savio,' Lalli said, 'but there's more. He was tense because he was going to be murdered.'

'He couldn't have known that!' I gasped.

'Not literally, no, but he had a definite perception of danger.'

'What could be dangerous about *blouses*?'

'Exactly what we're going to find out.'

The show was in the same building.

We walked past the sunlit garden into the atrium now milling with the press.

Waiters in white flitted about with finger foods. The bar was crowded already. Hidden speakers played music at a stealthy reptilian crawl. I lost Lalli, then spotted her across the room, deep in conversation with a journalist. She waved me over, and we joined the queue at the entrance.

The hall was filling up. Shukla and Savio were nowhere in sight. Lalli and I had premium seats between the man from *GQ* and the woman from *Vogue*.

The music swelled, the lights brightened and Xander, now in a black tux, and looking like an elderly penguin, held out his arms to us.

'At last my friends, I give you the essence of the Indian woman, in all her eight moods!'

Ila Arun lambasting *Choli ke peechay kya hai* drowned Xander's nasal whine as the introductory walk began with eight models doing a quick march that registered only as a brilliant blur.

'Damn! I hope I don't miss it,' Lalli murmured.

'What?'

'The right blouse.'

I had no idea what she meant, but I pointed out to her that there were four blouses to each name in the book. And each name was a look, not a woman. Mangl, Svetta, Zharin, Eshvarya, Joti, Anjli, Vendi, Saleen, Vylit, Pael. Here they all were, and they were fabulous.

All the blouses were worn with black. Black saris, black pants, black minis, maxis, gowns—as if what came after the blouse didn't matter. And it didn't, because those blouses were all we saw. They were elegant, seductive, delicate and sassy, but above all they had that near impossible quality in couture— they were *wearable*.

I hadn't heard a murmur from Lalli, and I turned, expecting to see her entranced.

She wasn't there. The seat next to me was empty.

But now there was a flare of music and the final round caught up momentum.

A beautifully choreographed rainbow fanned out as all eight models stepped out one after the other from behind a central black figure till they were arranged like a corolla around her. The lights went out for a blink.

When they came on again, the models had vanished.

'Ladies and gentlemen, the artist!'

The voice was unmistakably Lalli's. She couldn't possibly have grabbed the mic. I couldn't see her anywhere.

The audience rose as the models sashayed in, and then, the applause stopped, throttled in mid-clap.

Between the models strutting on the ramp, trotted one very bewildered man. He was elderly, with a greying beard and a stoop. Uneasy, hesitant, peering anxiously beyond the crowd, he looked ready to bolt.

And then I caught sight of Lalli.

She joined them on the ramp and addressed the hall. 'Ladies and gentlemen, it's my privilege to introduce the designer of the marvellous collection we've just viewed—Hussain Mohammad Afghani.'

There was a long moment of silence. Then the women on the ramp began clapping, and the audience responded. Uncertainly at first, then, as Hussain Afghani bowed, with mad enthusiasm.

Lalli held up a hand for silence.

'And I have the story right here for you. Mr Afghani will take questions later, but you must excuse him now.'

It was a strange statement to make, but the absolute authority in Lalli's calm voice brooked no questions.

She waited a few moments after Hussain Afghani had disappeared.

She met my eyes with that clear look that I find impossible to fathom.

'This collection, ladies and gentlemen, like all the previous couture presented under the label of Xander was designed and executed to the last detail by the man you just met. Hussain Mohammad Afghani. Xander merely knew him as Masterji, the man whom he paid a pittance every month, ostensibly for piece work, but in reality to get him to design all the garments in his couture line. The reason why Hussain Afghani is not here to tell you the story himself is a painful one. As I speak, Mr Afghani is being informed of the death of his son Imran. Ladies and gentlemen, keep your cameras ready. Inspector Savio and Inspector Shukla will shortly escort Xander and Xara into the police van parked at the front gate. They have confessed to the murder of Imran Afghani whose body was found this morning in the studio upstairs. And now, if you want pictures, hurry up and clear the hall.'

The hall was empty except for the two of us.

Something about Lalli kept me silent. She still looked as if coiled to spring.

Kale came in, escorting Hussain Afghani who seemed to have shrunk to half his size. He permitted Kale to steer him to a chair.

Lalli reached over and took the notebook from me. I'd forgotten I was still clutching it.

'So Imran had decided to fight for your rights,' she said.

He looked at her as though seeing her for the first time. 'You spoke to him? You met Imran?'

'No. But I saw this book.'

'How did you know about Imran? You met me at the gate and brought me in here, made me go on the ramp. You told everybody that this was my work on show. How did you know that? Who told you?'

'This book.'

'Eh? It only has some patterns.'

'No. It has the story of your life. A life of talent unrecognized. You endured years of injustice to give your son a good education.'

'English medium. From the first standard he studied in English medium. Study well, I told him, let the old things be, you must look ahead, make your life. And he made it too. Graduate. Good job. He was taking law classes after work.'

'And that made him aware of how you were being cheated. All the couture designs were yours. Xander was making huge amounts of money on your work.'

'Lakhs. Everything he sold ran into lakhs. You know how much he paid me?'

'I can imagine. Imran would not let this collection pass without your getting your due. It was a very important collection for Xander. The international press was invited for the viewing. Imran decided you should get full credit for it. It was not just the money. He was angry that your work was making someone else famous.'

'Red carpet gown? You saw that one? Everybody saw it on TV. That was mine.'

'I thought as much when I saw the purple blouse today.'

'Quite right. Same cut. You have a clear eye.'

'So you sent Imran here yesterday. He didn't return home.'

'We were worried all night. I tried Xander's phone, it was switched off. Since morning we have been running here and there, but who would have thought this would happen. Ya Allah!' He held his head in his hands and groaned. 'I must see him now. Take me to him now.'

'The jeep will be back here soon for you. What was Imran's plan?'

'I told him don't make a commotion. Ask to see Xander in his office. Speak politely. Tell him I will not tolerate injustice anymore.'

'I don't think that went according to plan. Xara met him in the office while fittings were going on in the studio. I think Imran told her he would not keep quiet about this show unless you got the credit for it. He probably threatened to go to the press. Xara asked him to wait till the rehearsal was over. After everyone had left, she took him up to the studio. She may have been either wearing the blouse she was to model, or else she had it with her, because Imran noticed it. She brought him some tea and said Xander would be along very soon. The tea was drugged. Once Imran was doped, the two of them bound him to the chair and planned their next step. I know Xander was there too because of the Scrabble board—'

'He's always doing that. It's second nature to him. He has to fiddle with those tiles first before he does anything,' Hussain broke in. 'He used to make fun of me in the early years because I didn't speak English. Gradually I picked up a few words from the game.'

'Enough to write up some notes on your work for Imran.'

'The book, yes. The book must have made Xander angry.'

'Perhaps it did. Nobody but the two of them

knew Imran was there. Nobody had seen him come in except Xara. They thought that was enough protection. So they left Imran doped and tied up, and locked the studio door. They went home, then went to a party. On the way home, they stopped by here. It was a little after midnight. Xander went up to the studio, strangled Imran who was still doped, locked the studio and had a good night's sleep. The next day he smashed the flimsy lock, "discovered" the body and called the police after first phoning a friendly politician. That's all he needed to do. Xander and Xara had their story ready. The police took away the body, they were free to get on with the show. Had you turned up to enquire after Imran, Xander would have told you he didn't even know you had a son. But the dead always make sure of justice. Do you know Imran left us a message? That's how we solved the case.'

'Really?'

'Kale, did you bring it? Thanks—see this blouse Hussain bhai, whom did you make it for?'

Hussain picked up the delicate green silk as if it was a strange object he'd never seen before. It was a warm olive green, with sleeves of a darker shade and tiny gold tassels edging the elegant geometry of the back.

He smoothed it thoughtfully, and handed it back with a sigh.

'Xara. It was made for Xara.'

'And Imran told us that. He woke up for a bit before Xander got there, and even in that drugged state, he tried his best to let us know what had happened. I think he knew by then that he was doomed. He tried to write a message—his pen didn't work. So he used Scrabble. He made up words that told us the story. Three words. *Olive. Bust. Tea.*'

Hussain drew in his breath sharply. 'He meant to say the woman in the blouse with the olive bust had drugged his tea.'

'Exactly. When I found Xara modelling the olive blouse, I knew it was she who had drugged and bound Imran. I knew the person who strangled Imran could be none other than Xander for two reasons. First, he cut off Imran's nails because they offended his eye. Second, he noticed the words Imran had made on the Scrabble board. Any other person would have simply swept the tiles back into the box. But this murderer acted true to character. He made up more words to distract the eye and left the board there.'

'He cut Imran's nails?' That last outrage overcame Hussain. He broke down, sobbing out his son's name.

We heard the jeep draw up at the gate. Kale helped Hussain to his feet. As he was leaving, he stopped as though struck by a sudden thought.

He turned to Lalli, and his features hardened.

'Why didn't you tell me all this to begin with?' he snarled. 'Why make me go up on the ramp and listen to applause when my son was lying dead? How could you even think that mattered to me?'

Lalli met his angry eyes with calm. 'I didn't think it mattered in the least to you, Hussain Bhai. But it was important to Imran. It was what he came here to accomplish. My deal is with the dead. I had to finish what Imran came here to do, and yes, that was very important to me.'

Suicide Point

For
Joe and Louise Burke

I first met Teddy during the Sada Suhagan affair. He was irresistible.

Imagine a mildly dishevelled James Bond—the first one, of course—sulking across the room. Every time I looked up, he met my eye, a ghazal in his glance. As he walked over, his smile unfolded like a sonnet, every feature iambic with intelligence. The lip's conclusive curve came as coda to discovery. Up close, his eyes melted like chocolate.

And all this before he'd even said a word. When he finally said hello, the word was a First Act entire.

'It comes off at night,' Savio muttered. I didn't need that warning. Teddy was simply too theatre to be true.

Teddy hadn't seen the inside of a theatre in years. Lalli was to blame for that. Ten years ago, he was out of work, dead broke and soaked to the gills when she suggested the police might have use for his talents. That started off a career that paid well, and dressed better. Over the years he'd become a reliable mole in the world of old money. It was a world that was shrinking fast. These days, Teddy was often out of a job.

He dropped by occasionally. I found him elusive,

and, despite the skilled flirting, rather dull. Lalli humoured him, Dr Q loathed him, and Shukla, I suspect, took notes. Savio ignored him.

Lalli always had a small package to give him as he left. His face changed when he took it from her, turning inward and absent. He often stalked off without a word. Teddy's stories were always the most outrageous and colourful, but there was something embarrassing about him.

We hadn't seen him in a while when the Vice guys called Lalli on Thursday. Teddy was on the job when he had keeled over with a mild heart attack. Thanks to some expert stage management, his cover hadn't been blown. But on Wednesday morning, once he was out of the ICU, Teddy vanished. His watch, wallet, car keys were at his bedside. The BMW was in the parking lot. The props were all there, but the man was gone.

The Vice guys had nothing further to report. They told Lalli all this with the air of handing over charge. Teddy was no longer in their employ. They didn't deal with Missing Persons.

The next day brought a letter:

Lalli—

Thanks for everything. I'm off to Suicide Point. You'll understand, you always do.

T

Lalli had no doubt Teddy had written it. Postmarked 3 p.m., the previous day, at Bandra Post Office. It had taken twenty-four hours to travel the five kilometres to our doorstep. Speed Post, true, but what kind of guy sends a suicide note by snail mail? It was typical of the man. He had lived taking everyone else for granted, and had decided to die the same way: Lalli was supposed to understand.

I knew nothing about Teddy. Did he have family? Where did he live? Who would weep for him?

Savio took the questions out of my head with another, more urgent one, 'You coming?'

Lalli was already at the door.

'I don't see the need for speed. The man must be dead by now,' I grumbled. One doesn't wait twenty-four hours, after sending a suicide note, to commit suicide.

We were silent as Lalli drove towards Khar. Past the main road, a labyrinth sucked us in. I was certain we were driving around in circles, but Lalli's stony profile didn't encourage questions.

'Next left,' Savio said suddenly.

'Teddy lives *here*?' And I had thought this was one of Lalli's famous shortcuts that would reliably surface at the right address. This simply could not be it. The seedy neighbourhood had given way to a slum. The rowhouses ahead looked ready for demolition. Teddy couldn't possibly live here.

'It's his present address,' Savio answered. 'This is Suicide Point.'

'Suicide Point? It's actually called that?'

'Yeah.'

There was nothing in view to explain the name. I expected some kind of cliff or crag to jump off—we were not far from the creek. Or else a tower of some sort, the shaky stump of a derelict fort perhaps. But there was nothing of the sort in sight.

Lalli strode away with a sure step, without giving our surroundings a glance. Savio, who has a trick of making six foot two of muscle seem invisible, effaced himself by chatting up the vendor in a little kiosk. The signboard said *Antim Bidi.*

I got out and followed Lalli. She had walked beyond a small mountain of garbage and landfill. I lost sight of her as I dithered over how to avoid wading through the filth. Savio cleared the dunghill with long easy strides.

It was a measure of my resentment against Teddy that I didn't venture ahead. I'm not usually persnickety. It brought back the feeling Teddy usually left me with—he invariably got me mad at myself. I was still working that out when Lalli and Savio returned. One look and I knew they'd drawn a blank. What were they expecting? A body?

'What's over there?' I demanded.

They stared at me. 'Suicide Point.'

'Sure, this is Suicide Point. But why?'

'Well.'

'Well what?'

Lalli sighed. 'Sometimes I forget you aren't police. There's a well here, Sita. It has a history. Every now and then missing persons get traced to this point, and then—pouf!'

'Urban legend,' Savio put in. 'There's no actual proof that anybody's ever jumped into that well. It's historic. There's actually a fat file on that well in Records. I went through it when I was a rookie. Two hundred and fifty missing persons traced to the well—and not a single body found. Last time we checked was about five years ago. At least once a year the chowki goes ballistic over it. But, it was the same in your time, wasn't it, Lalli?'

'Yes. It was a running joke. Four suicides reported in my twenty years, not one shred of evidence. It used to drive us all crazy. In each case the missing person had been sighted thereabouts, but the trail went cold. After each alarm we'd cover the well, and fat lot of good that did!'

'It came up again last year at the Annual, but for just the opposite reason. Some developer applied for landfill, and there was a hue and cry from the residents. They actually staged a dharna at the well. It beats me, I thought they'd jump at the chance of getting rid of the well,' Savio added.

'People love their horrors,' I said. 'Would we have so many superstitions otherwise? Did you say *residents*? People *live* at Suicide Point?' I couldn't believe anybody would want to live in a place with that kind of reputation.

'What did you think these houses are for? Didn't you see the merchandise at Antim Bidi? Business is flourishing.'

'I give up,' I muttered. 'People will live anywhere in this city, any hole in any wall.'

'I know quite a few who do live exactly like that,' Lalli said with a shade of asperity. 'Once it was considered Bombay's strength, not its weakness. Now I suppose we'll go the way of Delhi, with two million vanished overnight.'

'Two million! Lalli, you exaggerate.'

'Do I? I don't know about Delhi, but that's the number of homeless in our city. People who live where they can—on pavements, traffic islands, holes in the walls.'

On the drive home, I was silent, counting. On that brief drive I counted more than two hundred homeless on the street. If they vanished, would we be looking for them the way we were looking for Teddy?

Lalli turned to me and said abruptly, 'He's a friend, Sita.' It spooks me when she reads my mind.

It turned out they hadn't been expecting a body. They expected nothing—in keeping with tradition. But the least they could do was look. Savio promised to have the well uncovered and the police would have the customary exploration done.

There was no further news from the police. Teddy's flat (he had a 1 BHK in Mahim) was neat but reticent. He left no family. Women had infested his multiple lives, but he had never, to anybody's knowledge, pursued any relationship out of character.

So who was Teddy when he was at home? I was pondering over this when another letter turned up.

Ordinary post this time—an envelope with an enclosure. Postmarked at Bandra Post Office at 11 a.m.—three hours *before* he posted the suicide note. Lalli tore it open. A small pebble tumbled out. A strip of paper, carelessly torn from a notebook, had three words in Teddy's writing: *Death closes all.*

I backed off from the table, terrified. I didn't want to make sense of it. I just wanted out.

'Sit down, Sita.' Lalli's calm voice didn't calm me, but I obeyed. She got me a glass of iced water and sat down next to me. 'It's a funny thing about Teddy,' she said. 'He had exactly the same effect on me.'

'He doesn't have any effect on me. This whole thing's eerie.'

'Exactly. Because of the effect he has on you.'

'He just makes me gnash my teeth at myself.'

'Yes. Me too.'

That surprised me. 'I thought you liked him.'

'Sure, but it's hormonal. I have to keep reminding myself what a rascal he is.'

'Rascal—that's indulgent. I think he's selfish and completely amoral—'

'—and it's simply not fair he should be so madly attractive? Pity he left the stage.'

'Or the stage left him? The story I've heard is that

you gave him a life when he was down and out and dead drunk.'

'He already had a life I knew nothing about, and now he has more lives than a cat. Funny, he was suicidal when we met—but all these ten years I don't think he took another shot at it.'

'Till now.'

I stared at the pebble, wondering why he had picked that as his last will and testament. The words too, inflated with drama, like the man himself—'Death closes all.'

'*But something ere the end, some work of noble note may yet be done, not unbecoming men who strove with gods*...I remember the lines from my schooldays. Teddy, of course, infused the lines with irony.'

'*Ulysses.* I didn't get it at first. I suppose he meant it as an epitaph. He really had delusions of grandeur.'

'Oh no. He had no illusions about himself. He was terribly realistic.'

'But if he must kill himself, why disappear from the hospital just after a heart attack? Actually, that's a foolish question. That must have been an introspective day in the ICU. He must have faced up to his wasted life.'

'Wasted?'

'Oh come on, Lalli. He was a complete wastrel, not an ounce of self-respect. The job paid him well enough, but he was always glad of a handout. Don't think I haven't noticed all the surreptitious parcels he left with. Food?'

'Mostly. They weren't for him.'

'So whom were they meant for?'

'He never told me, and I never asked.'

'Savio said he lived alone.'

'Yes.'

'What then?'

Lalli shook her head. The note and the pebble held no interest for her. She got up impatiently and went to the window. I picked up the pebble idly and twirled it on the table. It was a perfectly ordinary pebble, small, no bigger than a chickpea, brown, irregular, stippled with a few pores. It spun on the table, a dizzying twist of brown and black, somehow reminding me of a planetesimal.

'Sita, how many cases you've solved for me!' Lalli spun around, her eyes shining. 'I would have missed this completely if you hadn't done that.'

'Done what?'

She pointed to the pebble still spinning on the table.

'Why, you haven't even examined it yet, Lalli. It's just a pebble.'

'Listen—'

Puzzled, I set the pebble spinning again.

'Do you hear it now?'

'Hear what? All I can hear is the pebble spinning on wood.'

'That's not a pebble. It's not stone.'

'No? Well I can tell you it isn't wood. It feels like a pebble.'

'It's not as dense as stone, a little denser than wood.'

I reached for my pencil and spun it on the table.

Lalli slid her keys towards me—the chain was weighted with a bead of agate.

She was right. All three objects produced different notes against the wood: the pencil sharp, the agate dull, the pebble in between.

'It's bone.'

'Bone?'

'The left pisiform, if it's human.'

'If! But why should it be? It could belong to any animal—'

'From anteater to zebra? True.'

'So how can you possibly know it's human?'

'I don't. But Teddy knew it was human. He wouldn't have sent it to me, otherwise.'

Small, unremarkable, dessicated, Teddy's gift still looked very much like a pebble to me.

But Lalli was so certain—and she hadn't so much as touched it.

'Don't you even want to pick it up?'

She held out her palm and pointed to the inner border of her wrist. 'Feel this.'

My fingertip rested on a small bulge of bone, exactly the size and shape of Teddy's gift.

'Now look at your pebble again, and you'll notice a facet. Right? Only one bone in the body looks like a pea with a facet, and this is it. This one's left-sided.'

'So why should he send you a wrist bone with

his epitaph? And when did he read Tennyson—in his theatre days?'

Lalli stared as if I'd said something shocking. Then she said, 'Savio's likely to be at the well just now. Do you feel like a trip to Suicide Point?'

***

The place was swarming with onlookers as the salvage team dragged the well. Savio was at Antim Bidi, looking glum. 'Nothing,' he said, quite unnecessarily.

'I know. Get me some water, will you?'

'Madam, Bisleri?' Antim Bidi's proprietor seemed eager for business. Lalli bought a bar of chocolate instead, and we stayed on to chat as Savio went to the well.

'Do you think they'll find something in the well?' Lalli asked.

'Dead body? No. There was a suicide when I first came here. But no body.'

'So maybe he didn't die here, eh?'

'No, that one died here all right. The stench was terrible. I was new here and when I smelt that, it drove me crazy. I couldn't eat, couldn't sleep. Better get used to it, they told me, it's a suicide. The stench lasts for a week, then it's over, but you have to bear it for a week. It happens once every few years they told me, but this is the first time since then. This one, now—Inspector showed me the man's photo. Yes, I told him, he was here. He bought a packet of biscuits. Seemed hungry, tore it open and devoured it right here while waiting for his change. Next thing I know, Inspector tells me he is suicide.'

'What biscuits did he buy?' Lalli asked.

'Salties, ten-rupee pack. Ate the lot, threw the wrapper in the bin and walked away. I asked him if he'd like a cold drink, all that salt was bound to get him thirsty, but he said no.'

'He paid you with a fifty-rupee note?'

'Hundred. There were ten-rupee notes in his wallet. I asked him for a tenner, he said he needed those, he needed change. There were perhaps two or three tenners in that wallet, apart from the hundred. Not much cash.'

'Around what time was this?'

'Eight o'clock. Maybe a little later. Place gets deserted by seven. I close at nine. Say, the Inspector's coming back with dead-body water, I don't want it spilling in my shop. God alone knows what it contains.'

The water in the plastic bottle Savio held out to Lalli looked clear and innocuous. I took a cautious sniff. It smelt vaguely sulphurous, but that could have been just imagination. Lalli dipped a strip of paper into the bottle. It turned deep blue.

'Is there a tubewell here close by? A hand pump?' Lalli asked Antim Bidi.

'Sure, at my place.'

'Can you get us some water from your pump? We'll watch the shop for you.'

He hurried away.

As expected, no customers approached the kiosk.

Lalli gave Savio my pebble and I was quite disconcerted to hear him ask, 'Wrist bone? One of those carpals I can never remember?'

Antim Bidi returned with about a litre of water. Lalli thanked him and moved away with Savio. I stayed on to quell his anxiety. 'Does she think the pump has dead-body water?' he asked.

'She just wants to make sure it doesn't.'

It didn't. The litmus came away with a very faint tinge of periwinkle. Nothing like the deeply alkaline reaction from the well.

I hurried to give Antim Bidi the good news. He opened a packet of chips to celebrate. 'Just as I was getting settled here, this suicide business has come up again. Of course the well water's tainted, but once the poison gets into our water supply, it will be mass suicide!'

'That's a scary thought.'

'Doesn't scare most folks here though. If I had my way, I'd have the well filled up and closed and something big built over it. We had an offer last year, you know?'

'Really? It didn't work out?'

'Oh, it worked out all right, but just the way the dadas here wanted. They took out a morcha, didn't they? Bhookh hartal around the well. What for? I asked. Better don't ask, older people told me. You'll have to answer to Datar otherwise.'

'Datar?'

'Datar Bungalow. See that stand of trees? Directly behind that. Big bungla, bhoot bungla it looks like, but Datar family still lives there. Timber business. They own this land, own the well.'

'Big family?'

'They come and go, crazy, half of them. Young people are all goondas, but the old man's in charge. Nobody here will cross him. We hardly see him, except when the lorries come in, every fortnight or so. Timber business, as I told you. He has a big Ganapati every year. Everybody contributes. Nobody grudges that, I don't grudge that, small price to pay for a peaceful life.'

'So why do you think Datar won't let go of the well?'

'Who knows? They say it's sacred, some say it's haunted. All I know is that it stinks up the air every two weeks, suicide or no suicide. There's never been a body in there, never will be, but it's dead-body water just the same.'

Lalli and Savio looked impatient, so I parted ways with Antim Bidi and slid in behind the wheel.

'Where to?'

But Lalli was curious about what Antim Bidi had told me, and asked me to drive towards Datar Bungalow.

Bhoot Bungla was an apt description. The mansion—a word any less grand wouldn't serve—was in advanced decay. Several windows were boarded in, the roof of one entire wing was gone, the large garden was a wilderness of thistles. And yet the place quivered with life. Washing festooned the fallen walls. There were children about—an abandoned tricycle half-hidden in the grass, a kite caught in the hoary peepal, the shrill voice of an irritated mother. A chained dog barked its head off.

A door opened and a man swaggered out and glared at us belligerently.

'Drive,' Lalli murmured, and we sped away.

***

'So what does it mean if the well water's alkaline?' I asked. 'Maybe somebody's been treating it because of the stench. Poured in bleach, maybe?'

'Why the stench, Sita?' Savio asked. There was a suppressed laugh in his voice that made me look around in surprise.

'What's the joke?'

He composed his face hastily. I couldn't read him—he looked both delighted and edgy.

'Too early to tell,' he muttered. 'It'll take a fortnight at least.'

'More. We might have scared them off,' Lalli said. 'I'd give them a month, Savio.'

'A month! That's bizarre! You expect to find Teddy's body after a whole month in that well?'

'Teddy?' they spoke together, startled.

'You don't expect to find Teddy's body in the well?'

'Hell, I hope not!' Savio said.

'We'll still have to look,' Lalli added.

For all that, they seemed to have abandoned Teddy. Savio got mysteriously busy, and over the next week, I barely saw him. Lalli, too, was engrossed in a mountain of files the Vice guys left on the living-room table. One morning she said Vice had sent the keys to Teddy's flat, and the least we could do was to see if everything was in order. It was her first mention of Teddy since our last visit to Suicide Point. I agreed eagerly, and we drove into Mahim after lunch.

As it turned out, there was little point to our visit. The flat was neat and completely devoid of character. None of the cupboards were locked. The clothes were classy, but worn. There were no books and no photographs. The pantry was stocked with a couple of packets of biscuits, a box of teabags and a tin of sugar. Nothing else. The fridge was bare. I sat in the forlorn living-room and tried to imagine a life from these props—and failed. There was nothing human about its tenant.

He had lived here with neither comforts nor discomforts, with neither distractions nor amusements. It left my question unanswered: Who was Teddy when he was at home?

The neighbour across the landing opened her door as we emerged and essayed a smile. 'You're his relatives? Poor gentleman, we miss him.'

'You knew him well?'

'No, can't say that. Very reserved. He went out early, came back late, Sundays also. No rest. No family. Suicide!' The chain of logic was complete, and she allowed herself a smug smile. Then her eyes turned hard and shrewd. 'You're family? Distant?'

'No. I'm from his office. There might be friends or relations who turn up, though. Here,' Lalli scribbled on a notepad and tore off the page. 'Give them this number, ask them to call me. They should ask for Lalli.'

'Lalli?'

'That's my name.'

We left her scrutinizing the scrap of paper as if it held the key to Teddy's mysterious life.

***

The police had lifted surveillance on Suicide Point. There were other, more pressing matters to attend to. The files went back to Vice. And so, over the weekend, the door was shut on Teddy's suicide. His unquiet spirit, though, raged intermittently.

One evening I answered the door to an unexpected visitor. A middle-aged man, spruce, scented, aglow with excitement. He ignored my questioning look and peered over my shoulder with an eager smile.

It was Antim Bidi in formals, and I had almost not recognized him.

He surprised me by greeting Lalli with something

akin to reverence. She, in turn, asked him his name. I left them to cozy up and went into the kitchen to organize sharbat.

'So, Pannalal, how did you find your way here?' I heard Lalli ask.

'Only yesterday, madam, I learnt who you are. From my biraadar. You will remember the case, he has a laundry in Kalina.'

'Fatafat Istri,' I reminded Lalli. 'Remember the Monochrome Madonna?'

'Ah yes, your bhabhi gave me an important lead in the case,' Lalli smiled. 'So you're from Banaras too?'

'Never been there, I'm a Bambaiyya through and through. Sometimes here, sometimes there, last five years at Suicide Point. Yesterday when I heard the story from my cousin, I thought I should pay my respects, especially as I have something to tell you.'

He set down his glass, and waited.

'I thought you might,' Lalli murmured. 'You struck me as an observant man.'

'Really?'

'For one thing you told us the stench from the well comes up every fortnight—and I thought to myself, I will hear from this Shriman when the stink comes up next. But you are a week early, so I suppose it's about the lorries?'

Pannalal's eyes popped at that. 'How did you know? You have—spies?'

Lalli laughed. 'Spies? You are my spy, Pannalal.

Datar's lorries come once a fortnight, and so does the stink—is that mere coincidence, or are the two related? You've thought about it, and arrived at an answer. So tell me what it is.'

'Madam, you are hundred percent correct. This is exactly what has occupied my brain since that day. It is not coincidence. The two events are connected. I've tried to recollect the best I can—it works this way. The lorries come in. A week after that, the stink starts up. It lasts about ten days. When the lorries make their next round I can tell the stink will subside over the next two days. That's the best I can do.'

'And that's a great help to me, Pannalal. One more thing—you speak about the lorries coming in. When do they leave?'

'Two lorries usually. They leave the same day. And about once a month the timber, all sawed and hewn, goes out.'

'So there's a timber-yard there in the bungalow?'

'Must be. But—'

'Yes?'

'It's silent. It's silent all the time. No sounds of saw or lathe. They keep it quiet. Datar has all his own workmen. They don't come out much.'

'And the lorries came yesterday?'

Pannalal looked startled again but this time he contented himself with a nod.

'You'd like the well filled up, Pannalal?'

'Yes.'

'Then you've done your bit. I'll let you know if I need any more information, but for now, forget about those lorries.'

'But—'

'I'll look after it.'

I thought Lalli was needlessly brusque and Pannalal looked a little bewildered as I walked him to the door.

I was surprised to see Savio that night. It was long after dinner, I was just about to go to bed. Lalli was already asleep. He cut through my questions and went to wake up Lalli.

'No, it's your case, Savio,' I heard her say.

'I'm not going without you. Five minutes.'

Savio caught me by the shoulders and twirled me around. 'Five minutes.'

We were out in two. Savio had the jeep waiting.

I thought we were going to Suicide Point, but he took a different route. We parked not too far from Danda. I could smell the cold sea air, corrupt with drying fish.

We walked in silence. The warm night settled around us like a cat, soft, breathy, inscrutable.

'We'll find the back gate open. There's a ladder up to the roof. Our man's tied a white scarf to the spot,' Savio said in a low voice. 'The turn's just ahead.'

I realized we were on the road just behind Datar Bungalow. The gate was open, and we slid in. It was pitch-dark, but Savio seemed to know his way. I didn't bother looking around, I just didn't want to get left behind in this spooky place. Lalli went up the ladder first. I followed, and Savio took some time following me.

We were up on a small terrace railed off from the sloping eaves. A white flutter caught my eye—the safe limit. I tried not to think of loose bricks and crumbling balconies as I crouched next to Lalli.

We could see nothing yet, but then, I had no idea what we were looking for.

We must have been waiting half an hour—it seemed an eternity to me—when lights blazed up revealing a courtyard beneath us. We were deep in shadow, in no danger of discovery, but I felt Savio's hand close on mine with a warning squeeze.

Men poured into the courtyard, there must have been a dozen of them. Several large doors opened on the courtyard. Godown or garage, I decided. The doors were unlocked, and two men went in while the others waited.

We heard a motor start up. A lorry backed out slowly. The men fitted a metal ramp to the back. Several large bundles rolled down. They were all bound close in sacking.

Next to me, Savio was recording every moment on video. I felt Lalli's arm quiver. Her face was stony with rage. The lorry, having emptied its load, returned to the garage.

Another door opened, another lorry backed out and out rolled the same sackcloth bundles. The doors were locked on the two lorries and the drivers joined the waiting crew. There was a moment or two of hesitation, almost as if they awaited a signal for the next step.

Then one man stepped forward and slit open the bundle closest to him. There was a lot of packing—straw, paper, cloth, all contriving not so much to protect the contents as to regularize its shape into something resembling a bale.

Two men bent down at each end of the bundle and lifting out the contents, flung it down on the paved courtyard. It hit the stone with a sickening *thwock.*

I didn't need to look to know it was a body. One more, another, and another. Eight in all. Men. Women. One was a child.

The bodies flopped, rolled, slid in the final debasement of human dignity. One man walked in and out of that inert assembly, prodding them with a stick, turning them over with a shod foot, jollying the men to get going, hurry up, hurry up…

Now each cadaver was being thrust into a thin bag that looked ghoulishly like a giant's stocking, tied beneath the shoulders and knotted at the head with a drawstring.

I felt a nudge from Savio, but mesmerized by horror, I couldn't move. 'Move, Sita, or we'll miss it,' Lalli whispered. Savio already had my arm. Between them they would drag me if they had to, but leave I must. Within minutes we were out on the road again.

'What now?' I asked, though I knew already. We were headed for the well.

This time our vantage put us at definite risk of discovery. Lalli had her arm around me, in either comfort or restraint. It was dead silent and dark, but not for long.

Here they came now, a man swinging a lantern at the van, and a silent procession of pallbearers.

I had imagined the place swarming with police, but it appeared we were the only spectators of this bizarre internment.

Savio muttered 'Infrared', stopping my question. He moved away deeper into the shadow of a shed for better vantage. Later, I found the images he filmed much clearer than the dim scene we had witnessed.

One by one the grisly packages were toppled into the well. Each trailed a rope that was fastened somewhere out of sight. We counted twenty-five bodies in all.

I had imagined that Savio would spring them, but no. They were still at it when we stole away. I was seething with outrage, but neither Savio nor Lalli would talk, and we parted silently to bed. At least, I did. Savio got busy at the phone, and Lalli sat alone in the balcony, waiting for dawn.

***

'So the well is a body dump?' I asked as we sat around breakfast, enjoying the brisk sunshine, toast-warm already at eight. I could do with a blazing sun this morning. Savio was still single-mindedly absorbing calories, but Lalli answered me.

'It's not a dump, Sita. It's a tank. Those bodies are being macerated in alkali.'

'Macerated? As in decomposed?'

'It's a controlled decomposition, to skeletonize them.'

'They're making skeletons? What for?'

'The bone trade's big business,' Savio said. 'And illegal traffic in cadavers is an international scam. Human skeletons are desperately needed in medical colleges. Students in hotshot campuses on the rest of the planet have been boning up off Suicide Point for years. Obviously, the Datars are a family business, going back generations.'

'But—where do the bodies come from?'

'That depends on the market,' Savio said. 'If the demand outstrips supply, things get speeded up. The going price for a dead relative is pretty high.'

'Don't hedge, Savio,' Lalli interrupted. 'Murder's the name of the game.'

'Why did you let them go then?' I was very close to tears—it was all so, so useless, somehow.

'It's not over, Sita,' Savio said quietly. 'We have to follow those skeletons.'

Lalli went to the bookcase and returned with Teddy's letters. She slid out the note with the pisiform bone. 'Teddy cracked the mystery that's had the police baffled for fifty years. He found this—he found much more, but he picked this up so that he could send it to me.'

'Then it's not a suicide note? Teddy didn't commit suicide?'

'He may have, I can't tell. Perhaps that's why he was so cryptic. Perhaps this is his way of saying thank you.'

'You'll understand, you always do,' I quoted from his letter. 'He was right about that, anyway. You understood the bone, you found the answer at Suicide Point. But how are you going to find where the skeletons are headed? I suppose your man in there will tell you when they're ready, and you'll follow the lorries.'

'Yes,' said Savio.

'No,' said Lalli. 'Teddy's already told us where the lorries will go.'

Savio sighed. 'Okay, tell us.'

'Death closes all. That line's in his suicide note because he thought I might recall the occasion when I heard him read the poem. It was here. He'd stopped by with a pile of school books. He was on assignment, tutoring the kid of a man under surveillance. He read the poem out with fine irony, telling me it was his homework. I think he ran into the people in that case again. Probably on this last job. He heard something, and the coin dropped. He was afraid he would be recognized—the stress brought on his angina—'

'But why vanish? Why not just call?' Savio burst out in irritation.

'How could he call, Savio, if he was intent on suicide?'

Muttering something about once a coward always a coward, Savio stormed out.

'Funny how much dislike Teddy's left behind,' I remarked.

'That never bothered him. It's Savio's case now.

He'll round up the operation, I won't be going back to Suicide Point. But there's still a small matter to clear up. I had a call from Teddy's lawyer. Apparently Teddy sold his flat two days before he vanished, and he's willed the proceeds to a charity. He had asked the lawyer to request me to deliver the cheque, so he's couriered it to me. Shall we go?'

The ashram Teddy had chosen as beneficiary was better known as the Beggars' Home, a sprawl of old buildings set in a verdant garden glimpsed from the busy road to Mahalakshmi.

Lalli handed over the cheque to the Superintendent. He took it with a puzzled look. 'Yes, it's all in order, but—'

'I think you'll remember the donor,' Lalli slid a photograph on the table. It was Teddy at his most flamboyant.

'Oh, of course. Regular visitor, at least once a month. Very devoted to our Mukesh, always brought a small gift for him. We haven't seen him in a while. Poor man—died suddenly?'

'Yes. Heart attack.'

'So kind of him to remember us. It will be used well, I promise you. I will make certain Mukesh gets everything he needs.'

'Mukesh has been with you long?'

'All his life. We get all the rejects, the derelicts, the incurables, the dying. Mukesh was about five when he came here. His family abandoned him in hospital when he slipped into a coma. TB meningitis. He's about twenty now. Spastic. Manages a few words. Goes about in his wheelchair. This gentleman spent an hour with Mukesh on each visit. Got a physiotherapist to work with him. Mukesh will miss him—he's still a small child at heart. He will be disappointed to know his uncle won't be coming to see him anymore.'

'Perhaps you could tell him his uncle sent this.' Lalli took a small parcel from her bag and laid it on the table.

The Superintendent smiled. 'Why, that's exactly what he's expecting.'

Lalli said. 'There's one more thing. You've recently appointed a man called Trimbak Joshi, haven't you?'

'Yes. That's right. Attendant. Any problem?'

'No, no problem at all. He's an old acquaintance, and I wondered if I could have a word with him?'

'Certainly. You'll find him helping Mukesh with his exercises in the garden. Mukesh seems to have taken a liking to the man.'

'Who's this Trimbak Joshi?' I demanded as we walked towards the garden.

'He witnessed Teddy's Will. There he is—look.'

Lalli's hand restrained me as I stepped forward. I followed her gaze. A boy in a wheelchair was attempting to throw a ball. It slipped from his uncoordinated grasp and rolled away. The man with him had his back to us. He was dressed in the ashram's white uniform. He bent to pick up the ball. When he straightened up, I caught a glimpse of his face. I turned to Lalli, but she had disappeared.

She was at the wheel when I got to the car.

'Lalli—didn't you see him?'

'Trimbak Joshi? Sure.'

'But—'

Lalli challenged me with an even look. 'But what, Sita?'

I didn't answer immediately.

I thought of the look on Trimbak Joshi's face. It was the look of a man who was doing exactly what he wanted to do. He hadn't seen us, but if he had, I'm certain he wouldn't have recognized us.

And we?

We knew the cavalier in the attendant's uniform.

We knew his other life—all his other lives, and we had given him up for dead.

Lalli touched my cheek gently. 'Let it go.'

And so we did.

Savio got the lot of them, Datar and his evil suppliers. The magnate who received the prepared skeletons and shipped them out was the man whose son Teddy had tutored.

The well was filled up, and tenders invited for development. There was a move to rename Suicide Point. Savio suggested Teddy's name, but it was turned down in favour of a local politician.

The police held a condolence meeting for Teddy, and his picture made it to the papers, at last. Sometimes, a man must be allowed to die before he can begin to live.

Murder in Seven Acts

For
Rashne

I. *The Incident of the Desk Ornament*

It was destined, I suppose.

There's no other way I can explain the immediate, and fatal, attraction I felt towards the object in the shop window.

It looked like—what? Definitely utilitarian, or it wouldn't be in the window of a shop that sold computer stationery, but its purpose was hard to guess. It was nothing more than a twist of some black shiny material implanted in a block of stone. And yet, it was nothing at all like that description.

It was a wisp of smoke. It was the very breath of stone liberated. No, *liberating itself.*

The black curve was sly with muscle, its subtle torque hefted with more power than the solid mass of stone below.

I couldn't just walk away.

'Desk ornament,' the guy at the counter said, and quoted an outrageous price for what turned out to be a tawdry strip of plastic stuck in some kind of faux stone.

I was still irritated when I got home.

The first thing I saw when I entered was the same darn thing sitting on the dining table.

And beaming with pride over its plastic perfection, was my brother, Vasu. There was a glass dome around it, imprisoning that essence of freedom.

'There, I knew you'd love it!' Vasu gloated.

'Desk ornament?' I ventured.

Vasu was a bit startled by that. 'You've seen it before?'

'Without the glass dome, yes,' I extended a hand to lift off that insult.

Lalli stopped me with a little scream. I then noticed a lavender haze within the jar.

'We're waiting for the Shuklas,' Lalli said.

'Plural?'

'Mrs Shukla has adopted Vasu as her brother. It's official.'

'Vasu, really?' I was deeply impressed.

My kid brother does impressive things with numbers and motorbikes, but he's low on heroics. Faced with a crisis, Vasu can put Houdini to shame as an escape artist. A skill I've often envied, when in the presence of Mrs Shukla.

Mrs Shukla is always addressed as Mrs Shukla, even by her husband. She is small and exquisite, like an enamelled ornament. Her movements are all minimal and precise. Her conversation is terse, her expressions literal. Her pretty face, mathematically defined with eyeliner and lipstick, is always tutored to a fatuous calm. Her eyes have the swift focus of surgical lasers, her small fingers are tensile as steel. All her clothes have the unrelenting drape of chainmail.

With all this, she is kind and affectionate, and has made up her mind to tame me.

This she does in small unobtrusive ways that she believes will, eventually, reform. She rearranges all small objects in my vicinity hoping their Euclidean symmetry might bully me into order and discipline. My overstuffed tote fills her with despair. She recently gifted me a severely rectangular handbag with cartilaginous sockets and a sclerotic tube for my pen. Its chrome corners are sharp enough to fracture a rib. She carries the adult version to work, complete with an accordion-like extension for dabba and fruit. Swung pendant, everything within its ambit is simply knocked dead. On the train, people fall back at her approach in a defensive crouch that has nothing to do with respect and everything to do with last week's bruises. In every way, she is the protective older sister my parents so intelligently denied me.

And Vasu, somehow, had acquired her.

I was still mulling this over when the Shuklas arrived with Savio and Dr Q. They were all here, apparently, at Vasu's invitation.

'What is it?' Savio asked.

'An object of beauty,' Dr Q offered.

'Object of beauty with iodine,' said Shukla the chemist.

'Oh, it's not iodine, it's sweet violet vapour,' Vasu said glibly. 'I know it's fading, but I have the smoking gun.'

'What is it?' Savio repeated.

'Birthday gift.'

Mrs Shukla tittered. Shukla turned red.

'Oh, I meant my birthday,' Vasu explained.

'Since when do you get two birthdays a week?' I asked.

'Belated. So I thought we could all enjoy it together. Dr Q?'

'Oh yes.' Dr Q produced a bottle. 'A soft rosé, as per specification.'

'Perfect, though I've no idea what that means. Now just a moment while I get my gun.'

He pulled out a mean-looking steel cylinder and stuck the nozzle beneath the dome. A very satisfyingly violet smoke spiralled around the Object.

All this while something had been bothering me, and I couldn't quite place it. Now I did.

It was Lalli's silence. Her face intent and withdrawn, she seemed miles away.

Vasu got rid of the dome and the Object was now revealed in all its geometric perfection as the smoke swirls faded away leaving a faint perfume of violets.

Mrs Shukla said, 'Sita, this is perfect for your desk.'

For once, I agreed with her.

'With Bhaiyya's gift, now you can write that famous novel at last,' she said.

'Oh no, Sita's not the only one getting this, all of us are,' Vasu interposed. 'If you're done admiring it, I'll fetch the plates.'

'Thank God, I was thinking Sita is enforcing some bhookh hartal,' Shukla said.

'No need to eat anything now, Shuklaji,' his wife murmured.

'Not for you maybe, Mrs Shukla, but policemen are hungry people.'

Savio agreed. 'Show's over, Vasu. Lovely, thanks a lot. I'll get the plates, but what are we eating?'

'This!'

'An edible object of beauty. What is it called, Vasu?' Dr Q asked.

'It's a—wait a moment, I have it written down.'

He took a crumpled scrap of paper from his pocket, and was smoothing it out when Lalli said, *'L'Oiseau dans l'espace.'*

'That's right, something French. I can't read what I've written,' Vasu crumpled the paper again.

Mrs Shukla picked it up and tossed it neatly into the bin. Had it been *my* litter, she would have stared at me till I caved in.

'Bird in space?' I ventured. 'What a perfect name. How did you guess?'

But she had slipped back into her abstraction, so I organized the cutlery unhappily. I didn't particularly want to digest my desk ornament.

Vasu, it soon appeared, lacked the nerve to take the knife to it.

So did the rest of us.

It looked like stone. And no, this was not plastic,

but some kind of gleaming hard material, surely guaranteed to taste like furniture.

Vasu was beginning to get that hunted look I knew so well. In the next few minutes, unless closely watched, my brother would disappear, abandoning the Object.

'Pity to destroy the symmetry,' Dr Q murmured.

Lalli was still in an abstraction.

'I'll do it,' Mrs Shukla grabbed the knife. Undaunted, she plunged the blade into the stone pedestal. It wobbled reassuringly and parted with a sliver of something soft.

'Sita, we are waiting,' Shukla said. 'We have eaten mirchi chocolate and namkeen ice-cream without complaint. Now it is your turn.'

It was absolutely delicious.

Its soul was potato—what else could firm up so well and yet yield so generously—but the 'stone' skin, so dazzlingly realistic, was also crunchy and spiked with spice.

The potato was a meld of the most basic aromas of pleasure: butter, pepper, and a faint hint of garlic, but none of these ingredients *showed*. It was as if the tuber had accumulated all these flavours in its long subterranean career.

Mrs Shukla suggested we saw the pedestal across, there might be some *stuffing*.

By now, not just Vasu, but Shukla and Savio had disappeared as well.

Lalli took the knife away from Mrs Shukla and laying the buckling Object flat, carved along the curve of the gleaming black strip.

Chocolate, tempered to perfection, encasing a delectably aromatic strawberry foam. A satin ganache veiled the praline spine crunchy with toasted almonds.

Dr Q, Lalli and I, trapped in the synapse between awe and delight, quite forgot the others. Mrs Shukla too had disappeared.

'Something's burning,' Lalli broke the trance, irritated.

Onions, with a nasty protein undertow.

I knew what that was.

The one time Savio and Vasu ever see eye to eye is when they collaborate on the only recipe they know.

It's beyond description, and is simply called 'bread stuff.' A loaf entire is sandwiched with everything they can salvage, slathered with cheese and onions, and incinerated whole. Rescued carbonized halfway between diamond and graphite, it's opened, still smoking, with a chainsaw. It belches out a molten lurch of cheese, and is devoured with a howl of triumph.

Dr Q firmly shut the kitchen door on this heresy, and poured the wine.

The wine was perfect, its fruity bouquet just dry enough to balance the decadent luxury of strawberries, chocolate and cream.

Something hovered like a gnat. Dr Q and Lalli

were absorbed in degustation, so it was up to me to respond.

'There is no ketchup, Sita,' Mrs Shukla said with weary patience, probably for the hundredth time.

Now that she had my attention at last, she let the shock show, each word enchained to a menacing silence. 'There—is—no—ketchup—in—the—house.'

'No,' I agreed.

'Shuklaji needs ketchup for grilled sandwich. Superb grilled sandwich Vasu Bhaiyya has made. Come on, let's have it hot. I'll run down to the store and get ketchup.'

I didn't stop her.

Grilled sandwich? If that was grilled, I was Helen of Troy.

And this Bhaiyya bit was beginning to get me.

Shukla appeared, 'Sita, so great cook in the family, then why not take lessons?'

'Mrs Shukla has gone for ketchup,' I told him.

He grinned. 'For what? Already it is consumed. But have no fear. Mrs Shukla will bring more bread also. She is always forethinking.'

'Shukla, try this last bit,' Dr Q held out a sliver of chocolate and a glass of wine.

'Cadbury is for children only, but Shukla will try the pink wine. But this is not wine, Dr Q. Fruit juice pure and simple. Watermelon.'

'Return to your grilled sandwich, Shukla, but send Vasu to me,' Lalli said. Vasu looked relieved when he saw the Object was almost gone.

'Good, was it?'

'Heavenly. Now tell us all about it.'

'Oh there's nothing much to tell. This guy I know, he's a chef, a molecular gastronome he calls himself, though it doesn't make much sense to me. He gave it to me. I'd worked out the geometry for one of his bigger creations. It kept collapsing till we tried this equation, and then it stood perfectly stable. He dropped by on the way to the airport and gave me this miniature version, gun and all. Sita, you can have the gun, and I've got you a book on basic molecular techniques.'

'You have?' I couldn't believe my luck. Very soon I might just have my own Desk Ornament—which reminded me of the one in the shop window, and I told them about it.

When they had all left, and Lalli and I were alone again, she said, 'Sita, the desk ornament has decided me. Tomorrow I must get you an Induri sari.'

I failed to see the connection, but the thought was delightful. Lalli's magenta Induri has long been an object of desire. Certainly, my luck was turning.

By next month, I might be a molecular gastronome in a burnt orange Induri.

II. *The Sensibilities of Sari Selection*

'Not everybody knows the right sari,' Maheshbhai said. There was reproof in that comment. He had not been here ten minutes before I put in a request for either burnt orange or green. He looked me over blandly. I could have been a piece of furniture, so ungendered was his gaze. He tied up the muslin bundle he had just opened.

'In that case, Lalliben, I must take your leave,' he said formally.

'No, no, Maheshbhai,' Lalli placated. 'I know you will have the right sari for my niece.'

'You are correct. I do have the right sari for her. But it is not the sari she wants.'

'How can you tell?' I asked. 'I haven't seen it yet.'

But Maheshbhai had turned deaf.

He opened his bundle again, though.

This time he took out a magnificent black and silver sari. I caught my breath, but didn't dare say a word.

He looked through me and handed the sari to Lalli. 'This is yours. Baby's is coming.'

'Oh, but I cannot buy one for myself now.' Lalli was stricken.

'Bas, then it is finished. I can go.'

'No, of course that's yours,' I said rapidly, as I saw my dream slipping away. Lalli agreed with a sigh. It really was perfect for her.

Under our adulation, Maheshbhai began to relent. He slid his hands deep into the bundle, muttering to himself and after some complicated manoeuvring, tugged out not one, but two saris.

I cried out, waking up Savio who was napping inside.

'Sita, all okay?' He came bursting out at a run, and sort of froze.

I had the first sari thrown casually over my shoulder. It was purple, the hue when mauve turns sullen and secretive. The coppery border reflected the purple and gleamed like a band of amethyst.

'Does it work?' I asked.

If they had said no, I would have died.

'Try the next one,' Savio said discouragingly.

This was sea green. It would turn turquoise in a waft of light. 'Both!' said Lalli and Savio in one voice.

'Not everybody knows the right sari,' Maheshbhai said.

'I can see now, it's an art,' I agreed humbly.

'No, no, not an art, not an art at all,' he corrected me. 'It is a sensibility. All the senses combined inform me this is right, that is wrong. You asked for burnt orange. I do have that shade. But I will not give it to you even if you paid four times the price. Orange will look wrong, taste wrong, move wrong, sound wrong, and say all the wrong things about you.'

'How true,' sighed my aunt, and I knew Maheshbhai's visit had nothing to do with buying me a sari.

'So do you still visit Manik Mahal?' Lalli asked.

'Who is in Manik Mahal these days? Nobody. Nobody at all.'

'All the old people—gone? Really, that's too sad!'

'And all this government interference, Lalliben,

has quite taken away my living. What prices they sell at! Six thousand, seven, for ordinary stuff? Now you know my prices, ek dum reasonable...'

Savio curtailed this bit of conversation by producing his wallet, and I brought in tea.

Maheshbhai grew reminiscent.

'From palace to office, from maharaja to karmachari. Kaliyug!'

Lalli agreed with a sigh.

'The stories I have heard! The glories! The generosity! The luxury!' More sighs for that vanished time.

Lalli said, 'Get that thing from your desk, will you, Sita?'

'What thing?'

I had just returned home from an insane morning at my old college, and hadn't been into my room yet.

On my desk was the Ornament.

Savio had a big grin when I returned with it.

Lalli placed it on the dining table, and continued listening to Maheshbhai.

He was now in mid-inventory of some dead maharaja's motor cars. Savio joined in with details. I hardly heard them.

Certainly, my luck had changed. By next week I would be making molecular boondis out of cabbage juice, swanning about in a slinky sea green Induri, one eye firmly on the desk ornament.

Maheshbhai followed my gaze and uttered an exclamation. 'Arre! That is Motiben's—'

'I thought it might be,' Lalli murmured. 'When did you last see her?'

'Motiben? About a year ago. Very happy in her office, but would she admit it? Oh no. "How does it feel after that derelict jhopda?" I asked. "Your mother will be happy today, rest her soul." She smiled and said, "Ba would have been happy were this Manik Mahal, but you see, it's only an office now." What can I say? Some people are never satisfied.'

'Any news of her since then?'

'No. Why do you ask?'

'Please, could you find out Maheshbhai, as quickly as you can?'

He took this in slowly. 'You know her then?'

'No, but I fear I may have to. Find out.'

Maheshbhai answered by picking up his potli, and bidding us goodbye.

III. *Gone!*

I pounced on Lalli as the door shut on Maheshbhai.

'Lalli, what's all this about? Who is Motiben? What or where is Manik Mahal? And why is my desk ornament Motiben's thing?'

Savio, my silent ally, looked volumes at Lalli. Unperturbed, she said, 'I've never heard of Motiben in all my life. Sita, you're so rich in plunder this morning, why not revel in your treasures? Savio, when I return, there will be work for us, so maybe an hour more of sleep will help.'

'Nah. I'm good for now, and better after Sita's fed me. I'm empty as a shell. I was up all night with the runs.'

'What do you expect?' Lalli shot back heartlessly from the door.

'Where's she off to?' I demanded.

Savio sighed. 'Five years of living with Lalli, and you're still asking that question?'

I got him his usual comfort food, a cup of cocoa and two coconut biscuits, and we sat at the kitchen table staring at the desk ornament.

Bird in Space. Apt.

But why had Lalli called it that?

No, she had called Vasu's molecular miracle that.

This was just a desk ornament.

'Gaad. I never will eat that bread stuff again!' Savio said with a shudder. 'Shukla looked so deprived, we made it for him. Vasu overdid the cheese. I'm not usually so sick after it.'

'You puked, last time.'

'Don't remind me. What did it taste like, that bird thingy?'

'Divine.'

'You know how Shukla is, he can't bear to eat anything fancy.'

'I bet Mrs Shukla drank straight out of the ketchup bottle.'

'How did you know?'

'She's in love with Vasu,' I said sadly.

'Nah. That's just the math puzzles. She loves *them*. Nobody loves Vasu, except you.'

'Now you're being mean.'

But I knew what he meant. Vasu has the annoying habit of disappearing just when he's most needed.

I had just completed that thought when Lalli returned, looking like thunder.

'Ah!' said Savio. 'Gone, is he?'

'Without a trace.'

'Timbuctoo?'

'No, it's Taklamakan. The watchman seemed to think the name very funny. Vasu left with a friend. Taklamakan? Who does maths in the desert?'

'It's his astronomy group,' I took up for my errant brother. 'They've set up an observatory there. But I thought he wasn't going till next month.'

'Evidently the planets conspired,' Lalli said drily. 'He could have told me last night. This is too much, even for Vasu.'

It wasn't, actually. 'What did you want from him?' I asked.

But Lalli, irritated, had stalked off to her room.

Savio got busy on his phone.

I almost wished Mrs Shukla were around to defend my brother.

Savio left the kitchen almost at the same moment as Lalli entered it. Their words collided too. 'He hasn't gone to Taklamakan.'

'He wouldn't leave without this,' Lalli held up a

small plastic pouch. 'It's his newest toy, a filter of some sort for astrophotography. He was telling me about it yesterday—and he's left it on my table. Why did he forget it? Vasu doesn't forget things.'

'Was he expecting you?' I asked.

'Yes! I spoke with him late last night. I didn't think Vasu would ditch me.'

Exactly.

I'd never say it aloud, but the only person Vasu will never ditch is Lalli. She's wise to all his tricks and, unlike our father, never lets on. That has earned her his loyalty.

'He hasn't left for Taklamakan. The nearest airport is Aksu. There's only one flight today—leaving about now. Vasu isn't on the manifest,' Savio said.

'Maybe he's just gone to the naka for toothpaste. He's always running out of stuff like that,' I ventured.

'No, the house is locked, with his usual placard.' It was Vasu's usual way of keeping in touch with his habitat. 'This time it says Taklamakan.'

Savio was already at the door. Lalli stared after him, her eyes wide with fear. I heard Savio's phone ring as he clattered down the stairs.

He doubled back to say the flight had left already, and he'd get after the guys at Aksu.

Aksu?

I didn't even know where that was.

Somewhere high up, the roof of the world.

Taklamakan.

The desert is a desolate place for a small boy to be lost in.

I had a sudden glimpse of Vasu's five-year-old face, his large eyes calm and trusting. For the last thirty years he'd relied on me to get him out of scrapes. What was I going to do now?

***

'We'll find him,' Lalli said briskly.

That called for coffee and we had just settled down with steaming mugs in the balcony, when the doorbell rang.

It was Maheshbhai again, but a very different man this morning. He had aged in the last few hours. He pushed past me and went straight to Lalli.

Sternly, almost accusingly he said, '*Off thhai gayu.*'

Dead, my brain translated.

I must have screamed.

I heard Maheshbhai ask angrily, 'What is the matter with this girl? Has she gone mad?' as Lalli hugged me fiercely.

Before she let me go, I heard her whisper in my ear, 'Vasu's all right. This isn't about Vasu.'

'My niece is anxious about her brother,' Lalli said coldly. 'Please consider your words, Maheshbhai.'

He apologized grudgingly.

I could see he was already regretting the purple sari. The sea green he had let go without much of a qualm.

I decided to patch up.

'So who is dead, Maheshbhai?' I asked.

'Lalliben knows. As usual, she is correct,' he said bitterly. 'Motiben died five days ago, just as you expected. You expected it, Lalliben, don't deny it. It was a heart attack. How did you know?'

Lalli pacified him with some patter before she said, 'I didn't know for sure, Maheshbhai. But I can tell you straight away it was not a heart attack. It was murder. Now tell me everything you know about Motiben so that I can find her murderer.'

IV. *Death of a Karmachari*

Motiben (said Maheshbhai), was first and foremost a karmachari.

From earliest childhood, her aim was to get a permanent government job, with accommodation and pension. This may sound a very strange ambition for a child, but if you knew the poverty and despair in which she was raised, you would applaud her.

Her father abandoned the family when Moti was eight. Her younger brother Bisu was my friend. She was like a parent to us, growing up. The mother was no use at all to them. Moti took care of the younger children, made certain they did well at school, kept them all neat and well fed. God alone knows how she managed. She stood first in SSC. That got her a scholarship to college, but she didn't take it. She took two years off to work jobs, this and that, to support the family, then got herself a degree through a correspondence course. One of these jobs took her to the Palace.

We still call Manik Mahal the Palace, but we were all born after the Holkars became commoners. We have no loyalty to those dead maharajas! Moti certainly didn't. She told us those old rajas were no better than our netas now, using their position to fill their pockets while the poor starved.

Moti read big books. We kids listened to her. Danga-fasad is no way to be successful she told us. The only way to win is to beat the tyrants at their own game. Show them how you can be important and responsible and still stay honest and honourable. We believed her. We tried, God knows, all of us tried.

We grew up. Life took us in different directions. I kept with the family trade. Some ten years ago, when I went past their old hut, I found it had become a garage. I asked around and discovered Motiben had achieved her life's ambition. She was a karmachari.

The family was still struggling, but they had a decent roof to struggle beneath! And as for Moti, she wasn't just any old karmachari. She was an important official in—guess where?—Manik Mahal.

She had often told us that her family belonged in Manik Mahal. I passed it off as a romantic notion. I don't think any different now. Still, when I heard of her good fortune, I picked up courage and made a visit to Manik Mahal.

She received me very kindly. Still the same simple and straightforward girl I respected so much. Truly, she showed us all the right path in life, but till today I have never paused to ask: Who showed *her* the way?

Nobody. It was all her own courage.

I wish I could say that her brothers and sisters live worthy of her. They don't. Yes, they are better off than they were, but you can tell immediately who's paying for their kids' education.

Bisu's okay, but the younger one, Pritam, I don't trust that guy. Always had shifty eyes.

I didn't think she would mind if I alluded to the old days, so I congratulated her, and made that comment that her mother would have been happy. 'She would have been happy if this were still Manik Mahal, but it's only a Customs Office now,' she said. At that time, I thought that arrogant.

'The one thing I have achieved is this room,' she remarked with a laugh.

It was a fine large room, but nothing great, full of cupboards bulging with files. Seeing my puzzled look, she pointed to an object on top of a cupboard.

Lalliben, it was this object. This fancy thing.

'This is mine by rights,' she said, 'and now I have earned the right to live with it.'

I never understood what she meant.

But a few days later, I noticed it in the shops. It's sold everywhere. I can't understand why she thought it so important. How much did you pay for it?

See? Cheap stuff. I thought so.

There. I've told you all I knew of Moti. Now let me tell you what I've heard.

Five days ago—that would have been Thursday last. Motiben came to work as usual. She received visitors in the morning—a lot of foreigners are always around, trying to imagine the old palace as they trek through the offices.

Motiben usually came downstairs to the pantry where they have a fridge, to take her bottle of buttermilk at lunch time. Other officers would have had it brought up to them on a tray, but she would have asked with a laugh, 'Since when are my legs paralyzed?'

That Thursday, she didn't come to fetch her buttermilk.

The attendant thought that strange. He finished his own lunch and checked the fridge. Moti's bottle was still there. So he decided to bend a rule and carry it up to her room.

He entered—the door was always open—and found her collapsed on the table.

She was dead, that was obvious, but they called the doctor anyway.

He said it was a heart attack.

Her family has been whining about the pension since then, that's what I've heard. That's all I heard. And no, I didn't look them up. I don't want to. They were never good to her.

V. *A Family Affair*

'I think I need to speak with Moti's brothers,' Lalli said. 'See if you can persuade them to come here. Tell them it's about the bird.'

'What bird?'

'Just tell them that. They'll understand.'

'And you expect them to come running?'

'Yes, I do.'

'Should I tell them Motiben was murdered? You haven't told me why you think so.'

'No, I haven't. I'm waiting for some proof. Have you seen this man before, Maheshbhai?' Lalli showed him the photograph of a bearded man.

'That's Pritam, Moti's youngest brother.'

'I thought it might be.'

Maheshbhai got up with a shrug. 'Okay, I'll try talking to them, but don't blame me if it doesn't work out.'

'I won't.' Lalli sent him away with a reassuring smile.

***

We got a message from Savio saying he was taking the next flight to Dubai, connecting to Aksu from there.

'Why?' I asked, mystified. 'Why, when both of you agreed he hasn't gone to Taklamakan?'

Lalli spelt out the dread thought. 'He didn't go of his own free will.'

'Wait! Vasu was kidnapped?'

'Yes.'

The bell rang.

It was Mrs Shukla. She thrust me aside impatiently and raced to Lalli.

'Shuklaji tells me Vasu Bhaiyya is missing. Please, please find him! I will die if something happens to him.'

'I'll do my best,' said my stoic aunt.

'You!' Mrs Shukla attacked me without notice. 'You sent him there!'

'Where?'

'Where he has gone. You must have asked for this or that and he must have gone to get it.'

'Then we needn't worry,' Lalli smiled. 'Vasu will turn up.'

Her voice rose dangerously. 'That's all you can say? *Vasu will turn up?*'

'What does Shukla say?' I asked.

'He is the same. You have corrupted Shuklaji with all your strange foods! He also said Vasu will turn up. And where is Savio? Nobody knows. As usual, missing in action. Who is there for Vasu? Nobody. Nobody!'

'You are here,' Lalli pointed out.

Mrs Shukla took this seriously. 'Yes, I'm here, but I'm the only one.' And after a few like observations, she left.

'For Shukla's sake,' Lalli murmured.

I was familiar with the sentiment. For Shukla's sake, she must be endured.

The house felt very Taklamakanish. Lalli wasn't talking. Later that night, she got busy on the computer. I heard voices. At ten, that meant a conference in a different time zone.

We were still waiting for news from Savio next morning when Maheshbhai arrived with a man in tow. I recognized him as the man in Lalli's photograph. Pritam, Motiben's youngest brother, was more than fair-skinned. He was pink from the heat. I put him down for albino, till I noticed his shifty brown eyes. He had a pugnacious air, and took his time sizing up the room and its appointments.

'So what can you tell me about the bird?' Lalli asked.

'Me? I came here because *you* had something to say about it.'

'I do. But that's about the bird your friend carried away. I hope you know you've seen the last of it?'

Pritam sprang up with an imprecation. 'Who told you that? It's with me, nobody will dare—'

'Is it? Christie's auction house called me last evening.'

'Why should they call you?'

'Because I had asked them to, in case the bird turned up.'

'But they're wrong. The bird is still where it was.'

'In Motiben's office?'

'Yes, it's still there, and I want it. It's mine.'

'Motiben also knew it was hers.'

'Yes, but I'm not like her. I take what's mine.'

Lalli brought the desk ornament from my room. 'And this? This was your idea, I suppose?'

'Yes. It was my idea. So what? What do you want? I've spent good money coming here, thinking you had something to tell me. Some way of getting what's rightfully mine. My mother was robbed—she was an ignorant woman. They demanded, she gave. They were rajas. She was nobody. But I'm not so stupid.'

'You are just as stupid, seeing you've been robbed too. I called you here because it's a family matter. Your greed resulted in the murder of your sister.'

'Murder? No. No!' The cry was torn out of him in anguish. He looked about wildly, then struck his head against the edge of the table repeatedly till Maheshbhai restrained him.

Lalli continued pitilessly. 'You knew she was against your plan. Didn't you tell your friend to go ahead despite that?'

Pritam had recovered his equanimity by now. His face grew sullen. He shrugged. 'I may have. She was my sister. Brothers and sisters argue all the time. This is a family matter.'

'Tell me why.'

'The bird is ours. It was taken from my mother by the royals. Later we found out it was valuable. That's when I made a cast and put it on sale. I made a little money that way. That too Motiben didn't like, but she didn't stop me because there was nothing illegal about it. She would have gone to court for it, but whom should we fight? They were all long gone. When Manik Mahal changed hands, the bird became office furniture. Bas, Motiben just wanted to sit in the same room as the bird. That too happened—but how did it help us? Many times I begged her to slip it in her bag and put one of these replicas in its place. Nobody would know the difference. "I would" was her answer.

'You must understand none of us knew how valuable it might be till I met this American. He came to Indore on some other work, I think, but he was also looking for the bird. When he met me, he wouldn't let me go, he got that fond of me. He took photos of us together. Met the family, brought sweets for the kids, American chocolates. I told him where the bird was, no harm since he was so friendly. One day, I took him to meet Motiben in her office.

'I had warned him to say nothing of the bird. But the moment he saw it, he couldn't contain himself. He offered us money. Ten thousand dollars. You know how much that is in rupees? But he didn't know my sister. She had him thrown out. That's the whole story.'

'Is it? What happened on the day Motiben died?'

'Motiben *died*. Isn't that enough?'

'Where was your friend that day?'

'The American? He left the previous day with his friends. Stopped by on his way to the airport with a big box of sweets for the family. He's a good man.

He's not a thief, and neither am I. He told me, Pritam, anybody can tell the bird is yours by rights.'

'I agree,' Lalli said surprisingly.

'Lalliben has your photo,' Maheshbhai informed Pritam.

'*Em*? Where did you get it? Can I see it?'

Lalli showed it to him. Pritam's face changed. 'This is not me.'

'No.'

'It's...*him*, isn't it?'

'Yes. It's him.'

'What should I do now?' The fight had gone out of Pritam. 'What did you mean by saying Motiben was murdered? You only wanted to scare me, right?'

'Oh no, no. Motiben was murdered. Your American friend murdered her.'

'Impossible.'

'I will show you how possible in a day or two. Meanwhile, here's my number, let me know if you catch sight of your friend again. But you won't. He's long vanished.'

'Wait—why should he harm her? The bird is still where it was.'

'Take another look at it, will you? If you'd like to know how valuable your bird is—a larger version sold for twenty-seven and a half million dollars seven years ago.'

'Twenty-seven *million* dollars!'

'You're forgetting the half million.'

Pritam nodded. 'Yes, you're right. For so large a sum, one might commit murder.'

'Get out of my house!' cried Lalli.

VI. *A Culinary Artist*

Maheshbhai stayed back, perhaps to dissociate himself from Pritam. I made tea. We talked saris, and then finally, we were rid of him.

'Let me tell you the story,' Lalli said.

She pointed to the photograph. 'It begins with him. Konstantin Brancusi, Romanian sculptor.'

'Romanian? But—'

'The resemblance is astonishing, isn't it? End of story.'

'Hardly! You're not telling me Pritam is related to a famous Romanian sculptor—'

'—who produced this famous abstract sculpture, the prototype of your desk ornament? Yes, I am. That's *L'Oiseau dans l'espace*. Twenty-seven million dollars.'

'And a half. So how did Pritam get it?'

'In the 1930s, the dashing young Maharaja of Indore, Yashwantrao Holkar and his lovely wife were the toast of Paris—naturally, with all the wealth they flung about. Yashwantrao was a connoisseur of the new art of the abstract, and he visited Brancusi in his studio. You can read all about it in art journals—I've been doing nothing else for the last two days. He optioned two marble versions of the Bird for a temple he had in mind, a very fanciful temple that Brancusi was eager to design himself. In 1938, Brancusi arrived in Indore, all fired up to carry out his dream project. He had made two large marble versions of the bird and a third one was cast in bronze. But the artist was evidently unfamiliar with the old warning, put not your trust in princes. By this time the Maharani was dead, the Maharaja was out hunting all night, or fussing with his motor cars. He refused to see Brancusi for three months. Brancusi accidentally broke the beak of one of the Birds, tormenting himself even more.

'Then he went home. But not before he had consoled himself with a liaison which ended in the birth of Motiben's mother. Brancusi probably carved a smaller version of the famous Bird for his beloved, and left it with her. And some time in the 1960s, when Moti was growing up, the Holkars discovered Brancusi had left an uncatalogued masterpiece, and claimed it for their collection.'

It was an incredible tale—and yet, perfectly possible.

'You recognized it when Vasu brought the molecular masterpiece?'

'I recognized the sculpture—I'd seen it in New York. This edible version was a work of art in itself. And then you told me about the desk ornament. Where did that come from? Two very different forgeries. That was curious!

'When I saw Vasu's bird and your desk ornament, I expected a small version of the Bird, exact in every detail, to show up at an auction somewhere. The usual purpose of forgery is—theft. So I put out the word, and started digging. My Induri connection, Maheshbhai, was a lucky break, but I did expect him to know *something*. Everybody has a raja rani story! From the art market, I didn't expect much. Most experts were sceptical, as Brancusi never admitted to making a scaled-down version. But Christie's called, and I knew the thief had pulled it off, with Vasu as the fall guy.'

'What do you mean?'

'Why not hear about it from someone who knows? Interesting guy, you'll like him.'

Our visitor arrived at eight, a large man who walked with the exquisite lightness of a dancer.

'You're not upset I said no to dinner?' he asked Lalli anxiously.

'That depends on your apology,' Lalli smiled.

He laughed and produced a small white box tied with a gold ribbon. 'This is for now. I will return for dinner another time, with a bigger box.'

'The best delights are the smallest.' Lalli opened the box and uttered a disbelieving cry. 'You remembered!'

He bowed gravely. 'I never forget I owe my happiness to you.'

Lalli dismissed that with a smile and introduced me.

I was meeting Arpit Maan, the chef. To him Michelin stars are as iron filings to a magnet—inescapable. The latest, he told us, was for his Tokyo restaurant.

'Now tell us about Indore,' Lalli said. 'I promised I'd only keep you ten minutes.'

'Oh I wouldn't fuss unless—'

'—you absolutely had to. I know. Indore!'

'The Culinary Art Show last week? Marvellous. Five years in the planning. The theme was Art Deco. We chose Indore for obvious reasons, but I never dreamt we'd be seeing something so spectacular. We had such an august gathering, but it was the young unknowns who stole the show.'

'Did you perhaps see something like this?'

Lalli introduced the desk ornament.

He smiled. 'The smaller version, how lovely.'

'Not really. This is plastic.'

'Oh-oh. Ours was—huge, ten, no twelve feet high. It killed me to have to eat it. What a work of perfection, an engineering marvel, really. The balance, the grace—'

'Yes, yes, time's running out. Who was the chef?'

'American guy. Fred Hawker. Amateur he said, but after training at El Bulli for two years one is no longer amateur. A magnificent creation. It was the winner, no two opinions on that! Techniques were daring and perfect. But the taste—ah. Orgasmic! He presented one large and two smaller ones. We demolished the large one. The two others, he said he would be taking back home.'

'Do you have a contact for this chef? Name, address, email?'

'Of course. Why? Do you doubt his talent?'

'Oh no, he's a genuine artist. We have, in fact, sampled his skills. But he may be a murderer.'

'Mur—oh my! I'll have to return soon for dinner and hear the whole story. Can I call and invite myself? Sita, will you be here too?'

'Oh yes,' I breathed. 'I'll be here.'

'The company you keep!' I remarked.

'Try the chocolates, Sita. You can't have tasted anything like this, ever.'

I hadn't.

'There's only one place in the world that makes these. I'll tell you the story some time. Never mind that. So you see now, how it was done? How Motiben died and the Bird was stolen? No?'

The phone trilled. We ran for it. Savio at last!

Savio's voice sounded windblown and impossibly distant.

'Found him!' he bawled. 'He's okay.'

And the line went dead leaving me with a picture of the two of them standing beneath the stars in an empty and featureless expanse.

It was another four hours before we heard from them again. Savio called from Dubai.

Vasu had been on that very flight Savio had checked—but in the cargo, shipped in a container addressed to the Astronomical Group of Taklamakan. There was, of course, no such group.

Savio had a hell of a time persuading the authorities

to open the container. They finally caved in when they registered feeble knocks from within (which of course Savio produced with his toe).

Vasu was lifted out half dead. Dehydrated, drugged, and near-demented with terror. Restored, he had simply fallen asleep.

'Which means I know nothing more,' Savio concluded.

'But we do,' Lalli assured him.

VII. *The Smoking Gun*

'We do?' I challenged.

'Of course, we do. Vasu came here with the smoking gun.'

'That evil-looking steel thing?'

'Ah yes, that too, but I meant it as metaphor. That exquisite sculpture we ate was the smoking gun. This American Fred Hawker probably thought the Bird was his birthright too. Hawker-Holkar. The Maharaja's third wife was American. The second wife (also American) got the Golden Bird, the bronze cast, in a divorce settlement. What did the third wife get? Perhaps she knew about Brancusi's liaison, and the small Bird. Fred enters the story—her grandson, probably. He knew about the small Bird, and he wanted it.

'He went for it in a daring way. A patient man, I'll say that for him! He was a talented chef, and there was a great challenge coming up in Indore. The

Holkars had a huge Art Deco collection, surely the small Bird would be the pride of it! He trained for two years to make himself an expert in the art he wanted to showcase—simply to steal the Bird. Vasu, in all innocence, helped Hawker with the balancing of the large bird—

'And so Fred Hawker goes to Indore for the Culinary Art Show. He looks up Pritam, whose resemblance to Brancusi vindicates the family story. He soon gets the story of the Bird out of Pritam. Definitely, Moti and her siblings knew all about their rascally grandfather. Pritam recognized the photograph of Brancusi I showed him. Finally, Hawker gets to see the Bird in Motiben's office. Unwisely, he shows his hand, and Motiben throws him out.'

'But Fred Hawker stays on to exhibit his own art—' I pointed out.

'How would he steal the statue otherwise? That was his plan all along.'

'I don't understand—'

'He makes three statues. One large, which gets eaten by the judges, and two smaller ones. Taking the smaller one, and smoking gun in hand, he makes a second visit to Motiben in apology. He shows her his replica. She is fascinated, and takes a closer look. He smokes her with his gun—some simple inhalational dope—he probably meant just to dope, not kill. He makes a quick substitution and leaves with the real thing. He doesn't wait around. Motiben dies, in one of those unpredictable cardiac responses to the anaesthetic.'

'No, that's not possible,' I interrupted. 'Pritam said the American left Indore the previous day.'

'No. Pritam concluded that because Fred said it was a goodbye visit.'

'How did Vasu get the Bird?'

'Just as he said. Vasu's skills get him to strange places. He was one of the consultants for the competition, online throughout. He helped Fred engineer the large Bird for the show. They met when Fred gifted him the small replica. Perhaps he feared Vasu knew about Brancusi's Bird. Fred had to get rid of him. They had got to be "almost friends", so Fred knew about Vasu's Taklamakan trip. Definitely he knew enough about Vasu's ways to hang that placard on the door. Again—an almost murder. He lured Vasu out into the van, squirted him senseless with the gun, and posted him in that container addressed to the Taklamakan Astronomical Group. If Savio hadn't got there—'

I blocked off that thought.

'How did the Bird get to Christie's?'

'Simple. One of Fred's culinary pals carried it home for him in an ice pack labelled Culinary Art Show Prize Winner. Once home, it was a family affair. Someone took it to Christie's.'

The Shuklas arrived just after Savio FaceTimed from the airport. Vasu looked ill, but happy.

'Mrs Shukla has planned a big welcome, hurry back,' I told him.

'Ah great. Got to go,' he said, predictably.

'Where has Bhaiyya gone now?' Mrs Shukla demanded.

'Home,' Lalli said.

After that starry night in the desert, where else would he be headed? Savio was driving him to Lonar.

Mrs Shukla drew me into the kitchen.

'Vasu went home to see parents before he saw me?' she asked.

'Natural, don't you think? He nearly died.'

'And how much I suffered? Parents didn't suffer, they didn't even know.'

'True.'

'So now I see you are both the same. Very nice, but not sensitive enough for Mrs Shukla. Not Bhaiyya material.'

'No,' I agreed.

Lalli looked pleased as she smoothed the pleats of her black Induri. I was not so sanguine.

'We lost him, Lalli,' I pointed out.

'Who? Whom?'

'Fred Hawker.'

'No, no, Interpol will get him in a day or two.'

'How? He faked everything surely—even his name, probably.'

'Of course. But not his prints. We got those, didn't we?'

'On the gun? But it must have been wiped down a thousand times.'

'No, not the gun. The scrap of paper he scribbled the name on. Mrs Shukla very kindly rescued it for me. She put it in the bin, remember, making you gnash your teeth?'

'Don't ever let her know,' I said.

'Of course not. But I've robbed you of your gun, Sita. Despite that violet vapour, it might still show traces of the dope that killed Moti.'

We fell silent, staring at the desk ornament.

Moti's embattled spirit hovered, straining for liberation, a bird in space.

Threnody

For
Marjorie,
In Memoriam

Thursday

Ponni Mami, Manda Tai, Hansa Ben and Betty, the matrons of Utkrusha-B, gather in our living room once a month to give Lalli a State of Building report. In my five years in Building, I've watched some of Lalli's more bizarre cases evolve out these Thursday conclaves.

I can recall quite a few offhand.

Betty's observation that Mrs Randheria of 37-B had a completely empty cupboard in her overstuffed flat led to the outrageous Mother Hubbard Affair.

Hansa Ben's tiff with Protomit Das over rosogollas made Lalli rush to Kolkata to trap an elusive murderer.

And, most recently, Betty's unsolvable Sudoku led to disastrous events at Vile Parle's most happening coffee shop, Cuppu Cheenu.

Lalli usually smiles dismissively when I wonder what the month will bring, but last week I found her more than usually animated when our guests had left.

The sisterhood had been enlarged by one. Ponni Mami had brought along her cousin Vedavalli, an elegant lady in her seventies who was carrying *The Triangular Hour,* and a well-thumbed copy too, for me to sign.

I liked her instantly.

And, after the initial thrill of meeting a reader had worn off, I still found her conversation interesting.

She was a good listener, and her observations were astute. We were soon chatting animatedly. 'You have the perfect life for a writer,' she remarked.

The poignancy in her voice stilled mine. Any reply I made now would be intrusive. She smiled at my hesitation. 'If you're wondering why I said that, it's because I had a very strange encounter when I was young—younger than you. It left me with an unsolved mystery I wish I could write about. Would you like to hear about it?'

London, 1960

Storybook London!

Isn't that what we expect?

I certainly did. I was twenty-three, and if not quite footloose and fancy-free, with plenty of time on my hands.

My husband worked at the Oriental Institute.

And Bloomsbury! Try telling a young woman weaned on Virginia Woolf it's a place like any other. It certainly wasn't to me. I expected the very air to smell of freedom, and gulped it in by the lungful, smog and all.

Looking back, I suppose I was in a permanent daze, near-paralyzed by cold and unwieldy clothing.

I was resentful of my husband, so smart and agile

in his three-piece suit. And I, leaden-paced with my woollen stockings getting my petticoat entangled and the sari in a twist, leaving me in a constant terror of tripping over the pleats. And then the clumpy shoes!

Oh, the pathos of it all.

It makes me cry to think what an idiot I was, I just had to tear all that off me and jump into a pair of pants, but I never did.

It's a paradox that continues to abash fifty years later: too scared to abandon the sari, I sought my soulmates among the wraiths of free spirits in Bloomsbury.

That's how I spent most mornings, drifting about the parks and reading, when I should have been working hard, making notes for my husband at the library in the British Museum.

Scholarship was hard work before computers, I can tell you that, and I was happy to ease my husband's burden.

The British Museum library was the only place where my clothes didn't oppress me. I floated right out of them into whatever tome lay open before me. Bliss, as I'd never known before, the world dismissed for the saner, kindlier, dimensions of thought and imagination—and I wasn't even reading anything I particularly wanted to. I was just making notes. The tables around me were dotted with men and women who wore the same look of exalted relief the mirror showed me.

From time to time, I did worry. Could this be limbo?

Such extended pleasure, such uninterrupted solitude, one couldn't revel in it indefinitely—surely there must be a price to pay. But no such demand threatened, and I wallowed unashamedly.

After about a fortnight I noticed one of my fellow readers, a tall lady with crisply curling hair. She was usually there in my line of vision. I caught her once or twice, observing me with a thoughtful air that I mistook for abstraction till she acknowledged me with a warm smile.

One morning, as I was entering the museum, I saw her ahead of me in the foyer, and quite without intending, surprised a puzzling tableau.

Just ahead of her, and presumably in her company, was a couple. There was a curious intentness in their step which excluded her. It was that, I think, which made me linger. My friend's usually calm mien showed perplexity, if not distress.

'You will take this, of course,' I heard her say. She held out a small canvas bag.

The couple stopped. I watched them exchange a look of exasperation. Then the man turned to her and said, 'No. We will not be taking this.'

The woman made a rueful moue at my friend, half apology, half triumph. I watched my friend assume her mask of hauteur again. I slipped away before she could see me.

I felt embarrassed as though I had ambushed them in a moment of intimacy—and after all these years, I still can't understand why.

The incident impressed me so deeply that the next day, when my friend spoke to me, I was guilty and tongue-tied. If she noticed, it only made her chattier. This time, we met in the park in Bloomsbury Square when I was squinting up at a statue. I remember, it was a statue of the politician Charles Fox.

'A bit of a rascal, I'm afraid, even if he did abolish the slave trade,' she observed.

I told her I knew nothing at all of British history and she responded with a refreshing, 'Why should you?'

She pointed out the name of the sculptor, a matter usually overlooked. I remember she gave the pedestal a familiar sort of pat as she mentioned the name.

'And what is it you so enjoy studying in the library?' she asked.

I laughed and explained I was merely taking notes, and it was the place I enjoyed, the peace of it more than the studying.

To my surprise, she nodded seriously. 'These are my stolen mornings too,' she said.

Something in her tone implied secrecy. I kept that in mind during our conversations over the next few days.

We usually walked in the park. I found myself telling her about my little life.

'Making notes for your husband isn't all you want to do,' she observed, and I confessed that I had a dream of being a writer one day.

It was an extravagant dream—all I had written so far was a short story. 'Tell me about it,' she invited.

'I wrote it in Tamil.'

'How does the language matter? Tell me about it.'

So I did, and regretted it almost immediately, as she turned thoughtful, making me wonder if she had even heard me.

Finally she asked if I could show her what the script looked like, and I wrote my name on the back of an envelope.

She chuckled, suddenly animated. 'It's a code, isn't it? Until you crack it. And then you wonder why it ever puzzled you. Can you read this?' And she jotted down some strange-looking marks. 'That's your name too—in cuneiform.'

'Cuneiform?' I didn't even know what that meant.

She shrugged. 'Just one of the things you learn when your husband's a famous archaeologist.'

It was the only personal fact she had let slip this far.

I knew her given name was Mary. Of course, I would have died rather than address her by name.

'You must have travelled a lot with him?' I asked.

'Oh yes, on all his digs. We just got back from Turkey.'

A few days later, she invited me to join her for a small picnic in the park on Monday. 'Right here,' she patted the pedestal of the Fox statue with the same easy familiarity I had noted earlier. 'After all, he's family.'

She greeted me with a warm smile at eleven on Monday. She looked particularly nice, in a pearl grey dress, and a lavender scarf with silver dots. She had a flush of anticipation too.

'My husband will be here in a few minutes,' she said eagerly. 'He's been in the country all week, his train should have arrived by now. And our friend will pick up the hamper from Fortnum's on her way. Today's our last day in London, we're off by the evening train, as soon as they finish their work at the museum. I'm so happy you were able to join us, I hope you'll enjoy yourself!'

Her happiness was so infectious, I already did.

Of course, by now I had invented a life for her. The home in the country was the sort they called a 'seat,' a great rambling place with flowers and dogs. The famous archaeologist husband I imagined as a frail man called Angus, with a silver walrus moustache and fierce blue eyes. He called her 'Gurrrl' and made her giggle. And somewhere at the back of the house was a forgotten room, where he stored his bagpipes and his kilts.

Here he came now. And oh no, he was the irritated man I had seen in the museum foyer.

Introductions were made and he was pleasant enough. He did have a moustache, but it was the sort easily ignored.

He looked expectantly at the horizon every few minutes, more for the picnic basket than the arrival of the friend, remarking he was 'peckish'.

We were chatting about the weather when she turned to her husband and said, 'Please don't forget this today.' And from the bag she had left leaning against the pedestal, she took out the same canvas satchel she had been carrying that day in the foyer.

He frowned, and would have ignored her if she hadn't urged him again. He said, with quiet severity as if reprimanding a child, 'No. Once and for all, this isn't one of your puzzles with a neat little solution at the end. This is nothing. It's about as significant as sawdust from a carpenter's shop. It doesn't mean anything.'

'Oh, but it does, let me—'

He put up his hand to stall her, then staggered suddenly, slipped and fell. His face had turned ashen, and his lips moved soundlessly.

Mary knelt on the grass, feeling his pulse, loosening his collar, murmuring his name in a heartrending voice. His eyes were shut, but his breathing seemed easy enough.

Just then I caught sight of a woman walking towards us, carrying a wickerwork basket. It was the friend, with the picnic hamper, and she was the woman I had noticed with them in the foyer that day.

As she caught sight of the recumbent figure on the grass, she broke into a run, and, almost instantly, she too collapsed heavily, falling inert and, to all appearances, lifeless, on the grass.

Mary, who had leapt to her feet at this startling development, suddenly froze.

She stepped forward, eyes fixed on the distance, excluding all of us. It was as if her fallen husband and the woman who had so strangely mirrored his fall, had both ceased to exist. Mary's isolation lasted probably no more than a minute or so, but it was so intense that it's my clearest memory of that day.

Then she walked rapidly towards her friend, and I hurried after her. Unlike Mary's husband, this lady was conscious, and responded to Mary's voice with a moan.

That seemed to reassure Mary. She straightened up, and taking a notepad from her elegant handbag, scribbled something on it. She tore off the page and handed it to me with a pound note. 'Veda, would you be so kind as to go to the chemist's—there's one not too far off—this should have them both recovered soon.' The assurance in her voice relieved my terror. Evidently she was a doctor, and would have them both on their feet in no time.

I hurried away. I glanced at the prescription as I handed it to the chemist and was surprised to find it was for eye drops.

The chemist frowned over it a bit, then he showed it to his assistant and they exchanged a smile. When he gave me the bottle, he said, 'Would you mind if we kept the prescription?'

Mystified, I shook my head, grabbed the precious bottle and raced back to the park.

Mary wasted no time in instilling the drops in her husband's eyes.

The lady was sitting up already, clutching her head. She was much younger than Mary, an attractive brunette in a smart blue dress.

Mary's next move was not quite what I expected.

She unpacked the picnic basket, and set the contents out on the grass, naming them as she did. 'Potato salad, goat's cheese and sage tart—ouch! That was hot! Tarte tatin, couscous, strawberries, chocolate biscuits, madeleines, muscadel—and *here*!'

She pounced on a small jar half full of a viscous brown liquid. 'Oh Barbara,' she sighed, 'not quite Fortnum and Mason, is it?'

Barbara's vacuous face, bluish pale under the powder and rouge, gave nothing away.

'You had best go home now,' Mary said gently, 'Veda will help you find a taxi.'

Barbara tottered after me, refusing help, refusing to acknowledge me till she was in the taxi, when she permitted herself a cold thank you.

Mary apologized, 'I'm afraid the picnic's all spoilt for you, dear.' In an uncharacteristic gesture of affection, she took my hand in a warm clasp. 'I've been thinking about your story, and I hope I will read it one day.'

And then she did something very strange. She

popped the little jar into the canvas bag, and handed it to me saying, 'I would like you to keep this. There's a story in here. If you can find it, write it! And—oh, don't ever open the jar.'

Her husband stirred, muttering as he awoke.

I took the bag from her hand stupidly. Of all things, I asked, 'What should I call the story?'

'Mithra's Trap,' she said at once.

Then her eyes rested for a moment on the man at our feet and a shadow darkened her face. When she spoke, her voice was low and vibrant. 'Threnody,' she said. 'That will be apt. Call it Threnody.'

I walked away.

Except for that jar, the bag was full of small brown porcelain chips, irregular bits, some large, some small, some jagged, some smooth. I emptied it on the floor when I got home. It was just—smashed crockery.

I never saw her again.

I kept the bag with its strange contents. I still have it. With passing years my memory of Mary has only grown more distinct.

I look at that bag very often. It reminds me of her grace and of her anguish, and reproaches me for not telling her story. I'd like to understand it before I die.

Thursday (continued)

When Veda finished her story, I noticed the others had been listening too. Still magnetized by her narrative, they leaned forward in intent silence. Veda said hesitantly, 'Lalli, I've heard so much about you from Ponni. I hope you won't think this an imposition.'

'Not at all. Can I see the bag now?'

'You've brought it here?' Betty asked. 'It's been what—fifty years? It's stayed with you all this while?'

Veda nodded ruefully. 'Fifty-five. Ponni, it's in my black bag, could you bring it?'

The canvas satchel was larger than I had imagined it, a faded khaki in colour.

Lalli took out the small jar and held it up against the light. It still looked very much as it had seemed to Veda fifty-five years ago, its contents now solidified to dark amber.

There was a smile on Lalli's face as she put the jar on the top shelf of the bookcase. 'Mary had very good reason to tell you never to open it. But let's look at the rest, shall we?'

I tipped the bag over on to the dining table.

Smashed crockery had been Veda's description: it was as good as any. The pieces were all flat, though. They ranged in hue from dark brown to beige, but they were patchily pigmented, as if the process of colouration was still in progress. They were so— random.

'How long will you be here, Veda?' Lalli asked.

'My flight's on Sunday morning.'

'Then shall we meet here on Saturday evening?'

'Oh we're all coming,' Betty announced. 'Are you sure you'll have the answer, Lalli? How could you possibly?'

'Oh I can't promise, Betty, but I think Mary will guide us, if we look at it from her point of view.'

'And how are we supposed to know what that is?'

But Lalli would be drawn no further.

I had one more question for Veda. 'That story you wrote—'

'Oh, I never went back to it. Life swallowed me up whole,' she smiled.

'What was it about?'

'A silly anecdote. Not so silly perhaps, because it changed my outlook. There—it's all vanished now.'

But her eyes told me it hadn't.

Saturday

Our guests were early. It was still ten minutes away from six when the doorbell rang.

Lalli wasn't home yet. She had left after lunch saying she would be back by five.

I welcomed our guests, hoping there would be enough small talk going till Lalli got home. But their chattiness soon fizzled into an agglutinative silence. They were here for the sole purpose of hearing Lalli. Their eyes roved the room. The canvas bag was nowhere in sight, but the jar was still where Lalli had placed it, and every woman's gaze kept returning to it. They passed up refreshments. Finally, I too surrendered to the general catatonia.

Lalli came in at six-thirty, looking exhausted.

I went to the kitchen to make her the cup of tea

she relished at this hour, very light and fragrant, with a twist of lemon and a bruised leaf of mint. Betty trailed me and demanded, 'Has she solved it?'

Honestly, I had no clue.

Lalli had not alluded to the matter since Thursday evening. Neither had I been able to sound off any of my brilliant ideas to Savio—he was away in Nagpur. There was so little information in Veda's intriguing tale, that I was sure Lalli had made no headway. Still, I knew she had been busy, working late into the night.

The silence in the living room grew even more intense as Lalli sipped her tea, relaxing visibly. Her eyes sparkled as she surveyed the room.

'Oh, you're looking for the bag—it's on its way. Why not hear its story before it arrives?'

'I thought you'd never begin,' Betty grumbled.

'Let's start then, Veda, with that disastrous picnic. Let's forget Mary for the moment and look at the other two people in your story. Both seemed felled by the same mysterious ailment, and at the same time.'

'Poison,' Betty announced with relish. 'That Mary poisoned them. That's what Benny says, and he should know.' She nodded wisely. Betty's husband, Benny, is a pharmacologist.

'Impossible. They may have been poisoned, but Mary had nothing to do with it,' Veda spiritedly defended her absent friend.

'Go on, Lalli,' Hansa Ben urged. 'Please, no interruptions, till we've heard Lalli out.'

'Yes, both of them were poisoned, and since they were afflicted at the same time, we can assume they were poisoned from the same source. The commonest source of poisoning is food, so the obvious explanation is that they had recently shared a meal that contained the poison. It was eleven in the morning, that meant they had breakfast together.

'But Mary thought they were miles apart that morning, didn't she? Her husband had ostensibly arrived from the country by train. Barbara was closer—she had picked up the picnic hamper from Fortnum and Mason. So Mary's husband must have been in London too, though he led Mary to believe he was coming up from the country.'

Lalli paused to let that sink in.

Veda's 'Oh-oh!', the usual Tamil descant for epiphany finally broke the brittle silence.

'You think they were together? The husband and Barbara?' Manda sounded disbelieving.

'Suicide pact,' Betty snapped. 'Dirty weekend, hearty breakfast, remorse, death. End of story.'

'I've never felt remorseful after a hearty breakfast,' Ponni retorted.

'I bet you've never had a dirty weekend either.'

'No. Have you?'

'No. Worse luck!' They giggled like a couple of schoolgirls.

Hansa bullied the meeting into order and Lalli continued.

'No, it wasn't a suicide pact. Because, and *only because* they had breakfasted together, Mary knew what had poisoned them. The two facts are linked. If you remember, Veda told us Mary had said they had recently returned from Turkey.'

She reached for the jar and held it up against the light, her eyes shining with mischief. 'Behold the Trap of Mithra!'

I let her down—she was looking expectantly at me, the bright kid in the class, but I was as clueless as the rest.

'Never mind Mithra. He's not in the story, whoever he is. Tell us about the *people,*' Hansa commanded.

'All right, I'll leave Sita to tell you Mithra's story later. Let's return to Mary. Mary knew the poison, so she knew it would be in the hamper, for where else would you hide a leaf, but in the forest?'

Again, Veda was the only one who got the allusion.

'The hamper was full of food, so it was the most natural thing to slip the jar in too. Mary found it. Her gentle comment, "Not quite Fortnum and Mason, is it?" told Barbara that Mary knew exactly how things stood.'

'But Mary sent for the medicine before she found the jar,' Betty objected.

'She recognized the symptoms because she was a doctor,' Veda answered. 'She was so sure of what to do the moment Barbara collapsed.'

'But not until then?' Lalli asked.

Veda hesitated. 'Yes—I hadn't realized that. When her husband collapsed, she was desperate, helpless. And then when she saw Barbara fall, she took command of the situation.'

'She took command the moment she realized they had been poisoned. At that very moment she recognized the poison as well, and sent you rushing for the antidote.'

'Eye drops? How can—'

'Atropine. In 1960, it was commonly sold over the counter. Quickly absorbed from the eye, it restored blood pressure and circulation, and revived Mary's husband. Barbara, who had recovered already, didn't need the antidote.'

'Mary was a doctor, after all.'

'No, she wasn't, but she knew a lot about poisons, and her knowledge was always accurate,' Lalli said.

'You talk as if you knew her,' Veda smiled.

'She also knew that the poisoning was accidental. The lovers had enjoyed the effects of their breakfast, and Barbara had slipped in the jar so that they could share its delights again. Mary recognized this jar for what it was—a traditional Turkish aphrodisiac. Call it Mithra's Trap, deli beli, plain honey or Turkish Viagra.'

'Rubbish!' Betty was dismissive. 'If honey contains Viagra, I should know by now. Benny swallows tons of it.'

'My mister is also very fond of honey,' Manda said speculatively.

'This is not the usual honey. This is honey from the Black Sea region, historically famous for driving you crazy. A teaspoon might give you a buzz, but a larger dose, especially in the middle-aged, can cause cardiac problems, even death. There's still a big market for it today. Mad honey, very, very expensive.'

Manda, Ponni and Betty exchanged breathless murmurs.

'We should get it analyzed,' Betty said with determination. 'Benny can do that for you, Veda. I'll take it with me then, Lalli.'

Lalli shrugged and left the room to get herself a glass of water.

'That was a lovely story,' Hansa got up with the other three. 'Really, it's quite late—'

And by the time Lalli joined us again, they were gone, all three, taking the jar with them.

'Please don't leave yet, Veda,' Lalli said.

'How can I? There's so much more I want to know. Threnody, a lament for her lost love…I wonder if she left him. Oh, I do so hope she left him!'

'No, she didn't,' Lalli said.

'You speak as if you knew her,' Veda said for the second time.

'I do. And that's why I understand her revenge.'

'Revenge? Against her husband?'

'Yes. The core of Mary's anger was not her husband's infidelity. It was his disrespect to her intelligence. She was prepared to overlook the first, but the other was insupportable.'

'That's a bit unfair,' I protested. 'He was this famous archaeologist and Mary was—'

'Probably taking notes for her husband, as I was,' Veda said it for me.

'Is that any reason why she should not make a legitimate discovery?' Lalli challenged.

'Discovery? That's a bit extreme, Lalli.'

'Judge for yourself,' Lalli said as the doorbell rang. 'Veda, I hope you won't mind the presence of my old friend Dr Qureshi. I can't possibly exclude him from this. Sita, could you run upstairs and ask Ramachandran if he would mind joining us?'

I got the door. Dr Q was in the company of a total contrast to his dapper self. The man with him was a giant in a torn shirt and filthy pyjamas. Clamped against his massive chest by one of the brawniest arms in all my acquaintance was…Mary's canvas satchel.

I heard Lalli greet him warmly as I slipped upstairs. 'Hussain Bhai, we have been impatient for your arrival.'

Ramachandran wasn't too happy to see me. 'What is it?' he asked crossly, still reading. At the sight of the tattered volume in his hand, I realized Lalli had invited the two most bookish men we knew.

Ramachandran came like a lamb when I told him Dr Q had been invited too.

'What's all this nonsense Ponni's been up to?' he demanded. 'She says Lalli's given them all some health honey. What's so healthy about it?'

I maintained a wise silence.

Lalli was in the kitchen, organizing refreshments. I whispered, 'The misters are being fed mad honey. What if they die?'

Lalli laughed. 'You don't imagine I'd leave Mary's jar lying around, surely! I switched bottles as soon as they left last Thursday. The bottle Betty walked away with was just ordinary honey—but we'll be hearing about its marvels very soon.'

When we were all equipped with sharbat, Lalli introduced Hussain Bhai. 'Hussain Bhai has a factory in Marol where he does bookbinding, but his real expertise is in the actual making of books.'

'Khandani pesha,' Hussain Bhai murmured modestly.

'He has restored some of my precious books so beautifully that I knew he was the right man to solve Mary's puzzle. When I took Mary's bag to him, I had already looked at those fragments from Mary's point of view. Dr Q, Ramachandran, Sita will get you up to speed about Mary's story later, but I want you to hear what Hussain Bhai has to say.'

Hussain had not yet surrendered the bag. He carefully parked his glass of sharbat by his chair, and walked to the dining table where he set down the bag with the greatest imaginable delicacy. I noticed Dr Q and Ramachandran exchange an approving glance.

We had all surrounded him by the time he opened the bag. He took out an object bundled in silk.

I recognized that silk with a gasp of outrage.

It was Lalli's most precious silk sari, the 'peacock's neck' Kanjivaram her mother had given her when she joined the force.

I had never seen her wear it.

It was breathtakingly beautiful, something to cherish and gloat over. What had possessed her to place it in that dirty old bag?

'When Lalli Sahiba brought this to me, she asked me how I saw it,' Hussain Bhai said. 'A bagful of broken tiles, I answered. Not so, she said, and showed me—this.'

He took out a sheaf of paper from the bundle and quickly wrapped it up again. He laid the sheaf on the table and invited us to examine it.

Sixteen sheets of butter paper, about sixteen inches by twelve. Each was a mosaic of bits of paper, a jigsaw puzzle complete in itself.

'When I realized what those chips in the bag were, I was too leery to handle them.' Lalli shrugged. 'So I cut out paper shapes and then I saw what Mary had. A basic geometry, repeating itself. I could easily assemble them into sixteen similar rectangles. Some of the chips had markings that suggested they may have been joined in some way. How? Why? What did my rectangles mean? So I took them to Hussain Bhai.'

'When I examined the broken tiles, I was too frightened to handle them. If anyone else had given them to me, I swear I would never have touched them,' Hussain Bhai said earnestly.

'Oh, I'm sure of that, Hussain Bhai,' Lalli soothed. 'But our friends here don't know what those bits are.'

'No? Ah, because the pieces are so old. We're used to fragments, you see. In my father's workshop in Taj Ganj, we had this huge sack of bits and pieces. Everything was in there, gold, silver, aqeeq, firdosi, markat—and of course, *this*. Ivory! To touch it is a prayer. No material is so beautiful to carve. Those days are long gone, but I could show you—see this.'

He drew out the cord around his neck. It was begrimed with filth and age, no longer recognizable as the skein of scarlet silk it had once been. Strung on it was a small amulet no bigger than my thumbnail. It was carved exquisitely with a design of antelopes leaping over a pond of water lilies. 'This is so old, we don't know which of our elders made it, but it is our work. This is just to show you I am familiar with the material, you understand? I don't do this work anymore.'

'Of course, we understand,' Lalli murmured.

'But the pieces you brought me are much older than this. This deep brown colour—it is hundreds of years old, maybe thousands. So ancient, anything might happen with one wrong step. I thought of how to stick these bits together. No question of using chemical adhesives, they may just turn them to ash. Then I remembered our old glue, the stuff we used for precious old materials, parchment, very fine leather, silk. Luckily, I found some in our godown. Making or buying it today is impossible, we no longer know where to find those plants. Saying Bismillah, I applied it in a thin layer, and Alhamdulillah, it worked! Soon I had sixteen rectangles of ivory. But how to join them? The material was so delicate, the joining would have to be done with very special copper wire. Once I had that, the rest was simple, and—here it is, Lalli Sahiba.'

Hussain Bhai flung back the silk with a conjuror's flourish. Nested in its lavish swirl was a *book*.

A folding book of sixteen ivory pages delicately hinged with burnished strips of copper.

A *blank* book.

A book I lusted for so madly, there was no crime I would not commit to possess it, knowing I would have to live out a million lifetimes before I found a word worthy enough to inscribe in it.

I didn't realize I had sighed till I heard Dr Q and Ramachandran exhale in anguish.

Hussain Bhai opened and shut the book several times, each time a knife thrust in my soul.

At a distance, I heard Lalli thank him. The others crowded him with congratulations and praise. I watched him wipe away his tears as he walked away, taking one last look at the object he probably coveted more than life itself. I heard him say, 'I am grateful, very grateful, to have done this work. Today my life is fulfilled.'

And then, there we were, staring at this object of incomparable beauty, one I too had dismissed as debris.

Mary had never seen it as debris. *This* is what Mary had seen. She had anticipated and predicted the geometry of a book from a sack of shattered tiles.

We had the story of the poisoned lovers, but what was Mary's story?

'Hussain Bhai's words are truer than he suspects. Making this book is a reward beyond imagination. All of us have been privileged to see this book because of you, Veda. I don't yet know if what I'm going to tell you next is true. Right now, it's my assumption. Even if proved wrong, it's an assumption I'm going to maintain for Mary's sake.' Lalli made no attempt to check her tears as she ran her fingertips over the ivory tablet. 'Knowing what we do about Mary, this might be more than just any book.'

'What do we know about Mary?' Dr Q asked.

Lalli addressed Veda. 'When you saw Mary hold out this bag to her husband, and he refuse it, you didn't realize what it meant. She was offering him much more than this book. She was offering him an electric moment in civilization.

'He had excavated whole libraries in Mesopotamia, you might argue, what could one book mean to him?

'Just this. The libraries he had discovered had clay tablets, each one the equivalent of a page. The concept of a book, the cohesive exploration of an idea, was as yet unknown. If he had let Mary show him what she saw, he might have had the triumph of claiming an unbelievable discovery—*the oldest book in the world.*

'The Assyrians had literature, myth and poetry, but all of it tediously inscribed in cuneiform on clay tablets, one page baked at a time. This is the first evidence that they may have already foreseen an easier way.

'That's what I think this is. That's what Mary knew it was. That's what you've cherished for fifty-five years, Veda. The oldest book in the world.'

We wept for Mary as we worshipped the book.

'How old do you think it is?' Dr Q asked.

'Between 900 and 750 BCE, I'd say. But my education's very rusty.' Lalli grimaced. I caught a flash of anger in her eyes.

'Will you—' Dr Q's question was so low, it was almost soundless.

Lalli shook her head and looked away. Dr Q's eyes followed her anxiously.

It was one more glimpse of my aunt's submerged life that even Savio knew nothing about.

'So this was Mary's revenge?' Veda said. 'This really is a threnody. That's a musical term, isn't it? She had a very rich voice. She was not a doctor, you said. Was she a musician?'

'I believe she was, yes.'

I couldn't stand it any longer. 'Just who was Mary?' I burst out.

'Yes, who was Mary?' the rest of them chorused.

'Sita, I didn't expect you to ask me that! Mary told Veda who she was. Remember, she patted the statue of Fox where they usually met and said, "He's family."'

'Fox? Mary Fox? Why do you expect me to know her?' I was really irritated now, more at Lalli than at my own ignorance.

'She was a writer, Sita.'

'I've never heard of a writer called Mary Fox.'

Veda's musical 'Oh-Oh!' rang out again and she hugged Lalli, crying and laughing all at once.

Then she came over to me and took my hands in hers. 'Mary didn't mean Fox when she said "He's family." She meant the sculptor. I remembered his name just now. Richard Westmacott.'

OhmyGod!

Mary Westmacott.

Agatha Christie.